D1456918

Blood
Relations

Also
by Roberta Silman

For Children:
SOMEBODY ELSE'S CHILD

Blood
Relations

Roberta Silman

An Atlantic Monthly Press Book
Little, Brown and Company
Boston — Toronto

FIRST EDITION

T05/77

Company and *Debut* originally appeared in *The Atlantic; Children in the
Park, A Bad Baby* and *Lost* (under the title *For Reasons of Health*) in
The New Yorker; Houses in *McCall's; Wedding Day* and *The Running*
(under the title *Running with Such Grace*) in *Redbook; Giving Blood*
in *Quest/77; Rescue* in *Family Circle.*

LIBRARY OF CONGRESS CATALOGING IN PUBLICATION DATA

Silman. Roberta.
  Blood relations.

  "An Atlantic Monthly Press book."
  CONTENTS: A day in the country.—Company.—Giving
blood. [etc.]
  I. Title.
PZ4.S57234B   [PS3569.I45]   813'.5'4   76-56749
ISBN 0-316-79108-3

ATLANTIC–LITTLE, BROWN BOOKS
ARE PUBLISHED BY
LITTLE, BROWN AND COMPANY
IN ASSOCIATION WITH
THE ATLANTIC MONTHLY PRESS

Designed by Susan Windheim

*Published simultaneously in Canada
by Little, Brown & Company (Canada) Limited*

PRINTED IN THE UNITED STATES OF AMERICA

For Bob

and

For my parents — Phoebe and Herman Karpel

1961932

. . . We see the people who go to market, eat by day, sleep by night, who babble nonsense, marry, grow old, good-naturedly drag their dead to the cemetery, but we do not see or hear those who suffer and what is terrible in life goes on somewhere behind the scenes.

— ANTON CHEKHOV,
"Gooseberries"

Contents

part
one

A Day in the Country

HE SLOWED THE CAR DOWN TO LET SOMEONE PASS.

"The last man to die in the Vietnamese War hasn't been born yet," my father said.

"But it won't be an American," I replied. "We'll be out of there."

"Maybe. Don't be too sure. And if it isn't an American it will be an Oriental, but it will be somebody, lots of bodies."

"But not us."

"Because you and Phil marched? Middle-aged fools, ponytailed boys," he muttered. "A country of marchers. Sure, it's easier to walk than to sit in a library and study, it's even easier to walk than to take care of your children. Better stay home and take care of your children. Teach them right and wrong. Teach them how to study. Teach them responsibility. The kids today — they're impossible . . ." His voice trailed off, not angry, just bewildered.

"But, Dad, it's so complicated today. The war ate into our lives, everyone got discouraged, the kids felt beaten before they began. That's why so many tried drugs. Now that it's over we can begin to live." I stopped, searching for the word that would make him understand. "We can begin to live normally."

I turned around in my seat belt to see my mother's face. Her eyes were calm as she waited for his reply. She knew what he was going to say and she agreed with him.

But he surprised me. He was silent for a while. I looked out the window. The Taconic Parkway stretched out ahead of us. It was the first weekend in June; we were on our way to the house in the Berkshires. Phil had left early that morning in our station wagon with the children. I had waited for my parents.

Finally my father said quietly, "You're wrong. You can't wait for peace to live normally. You live normally in spite of war, in spite of everything. Listen, Laura, there was a My Lai, a Vietnam, in every village in Russia when I was growing up. Do you think the Cossacks just rode around on beautiful horses? People were killed for being accused of stealing. Sure, Jews, but others, too. No trial. No nothing. Life was a constant threat. But parents didn't sit around wringing their hands. They brought up their children, they took care of them, they taught them to read whatever language they knew. If they couldn't go to public schools they made schools in the synagogue, they taught them the most important things were honesty, respect, love, the family. They didn't worry about a just God or a dead God; they were human, they lived as human beings, not animals."

"And got the hell out of there as soon as they could," I said.

"Why not? It wasn't pleasant. They wanted better for themselves and their children, but while they were there they remained human."

"But, Dad, there are so many more temptations today. The world is smaller, the family is falling apart . . ."

"Because you, all of you, all my educated children and their friends are letting it!" Then, seeing my face, he added softly, "Not you, Laura, you have a beautiful family, but in general." I sat back.

"Laura, I remember when the Cossacks were particularly angry in Olshan, they were tearing through the streets, we didn't know where they would barge in next; it went on for about a week. I must have been about eleven. Every night after our supper my mother would bundle us up and take us next door to our cousins, the Kaplans — you remember Lazar — well, his mother was a beautiful violinist, and we would sit and listen while she played for us, and then someone would read aloud or tell a story and we would feel calmer, and then Mama would hurry us back to our beds, and sing to us, sometimes for an hour before we went to sleep. Now all they want to do is play tennis and go to Acapulco and complain how empty their lives are or how they want to be men."

"Oh, come on, Dad, be fair." I laughed and he smiled.

My mother was so quiet. "Mom, what do you think?" I said. She shrugged and gestured toward the window. We could see the beginnings of the Catskills. Near the parkway were the prosperous farms of Dutchess County, which looked untouched by anything. The car glided through that peaceful country. It was another world.

"Remember the old blue Packard and how we used to ride to Peekskill in the snow with newspapers and blankets around our ankles to keep warm?" I said absently.

"Just blankets," my mother said.

"Newspapers, too. It's nothing to be ashamed of. They're the best for keeping warm." I was insistent.

"I only remember blankets," my mother said.

"You know, it used to take us longer to go to Peekskill then than it takes us to go to the Berkshires now," my father said. I nodded. We used to visit friends who had built what was really a commune. True communists, disenchanted with Russia after the Moscow trials, they had disentangled themselves from the Party and left their businesses and professions and built a small group of houses and lived by farming and odd jobs.

Every few months all through the war we would arrive with lots of rye bread and delicatessen. While the grownups talked my sisters and I played in the nearby woods. In the summer we picked bunches of joe-pie weed, Queen Anne's lace, gentian and goldenrod that would be tight in our fists when they bundled us up in the dark car to make the trip home. That commune looked hopefully toward peace. What they got was McCarthy, Korea, the Rosenberg trial. The only one left now is an invalid, practically senile, in a home for the aged in Brooklyn, all his bills paid for by my father.

"That blue Packard was a honey of a car. Not fancy, but it had class," he said and smiled to himself.

The last time I saw the Packard was in Ithaca. I had been at college for two and a half months. Someone called me to the corridor phone.

"I'm in Horse Heads," he said. No hello, no how-are-you.

"Dad!" My voice quivered as it always did when I hadn't seen my parents for a long time.

"Where are you?" I said stupidly.

"In Horse Heads," he repeated, "at a customer's. It's about half an hour from you."

"How's Mom, the girls?"

"Fine, everything's fine. Why aren't you in the library?"

"Because it's almost dinnertime. I just came back."

"I'll meet you in front of the library in half an hour and we'll go out to eat." Before I could answer he was gone.

My father had seen the library at Cornell for the first time when he brought me up to school. We had walked through it and when we got out he had said, "All you need is right there."

I washed my face and put on some lipstick and even tried to dab some powder on my nose. I had a cold and wasn't getting enough sleep. Then I trudged back to the library. By mid-November it's cold in Ithaca and from the warm vestibule I watched for the old blue Packard. He got out. We hugged each other. "You look fine," he said after a long look into my eyes. Then he insisted on going into the library. There were very few people there; one girl was fast asleep, her straw-colored hair splayed across the oak desk. She lived near me in the dorm and I knew she was working on a paper and I felt sorry for her. But he smiled when he saw her.

The next morning I had a ten o'clock lecture with Einaudi, the famous government professor. I could see my father wanted to go, and as I told him about it his face clouded with indecision. Then he decided to be sensible.

"No, by that time I can be in Elmira," he said.

He should have stayed. We found Einaudi hard to understand but my father would have gotten every word.

My father could have been a scholar, and in his spare time he had learned a lot about the Talmud and the voluminous commentaries on it. He had sent me, the oldest of three daughters, to Cornell to become a lawyer. No, a judge. In truth — articulated rarely — the first woman justice of the Supreme Court. I knew that night we had dinner I wasn't going to be a lawyer, but I didn't tell him that till later.

I had dozed a little and my parents were chatting. I smiled as I opened my eyes. My mother was talking about someone who had died.

"Laura, remember her daughter, Joan Dworkin?" she said. Yes, a tall nice dull girl.

"She married a doctor and they have two children — twins, I think — and she just got her degree in library science. You ought to do that, Laura." I frowned but said nothing.

"Why a librarian?" my father asked. "She can be a librarian when she's seventy-five."

"It's practical."

"Let her write her stories. What does she have to be practical for? Her husband makes a good living. Library work is boring. When I'm ninety I'll retire and become a librarian." He chuckled.

It could happen. His parents died in their mid-nineties of no apparent illness.

My mother, the mind-reader, said, "Dad donated a window at the temple in honor of Grandma and Grandpa."

"How nice," I said.

"The temple has a big deficit," he explained.

We had just passed Hudson. The next exit off the Taconic was ours.

"We'll stop at Friendly's for lunch. It will be just two." My mother looked at her watch.

"We'll eat at the house, with the children," my father said.

"Oh, Herb, don't be silly. The children don't wait until two to eat. They're out planting the garden. You know how determined Phil is about that. It will be easier to grab a bite at Friendly's."

"Why should we eat in a restaurant when we can eat in our own house?" She sighed. So many years of traveling, often for eight weeks on the road at a time, had made him uncomfortable in restaurants.

Although my parents usually called the house in the Berkshires "our house" it was really their house. Phil and I had found the land — a spectacular piece of meadow and forest protected on three sides by the state forest. My father helped us buy it; we thought we would build later. But when my parents saw the land they decided to build a house for all of their children and grandchildren to use. Phil had designed the house with an architect friend, and though I didn't know it till this very moment I was terrified that my parents wouldn't like it. My father was better than my mother, but neither of them could read plans very well. Her idea of a home was something with a center hall and the living room on one side and the dining room on the other. This was a striking, unconventional house. They had seen it during the winter when it was framed out, then once again before the windows were put in. There had been a huge scaffold in the main room, and the fireplace wasn't yet finished. Then they had gone to Europe for a month.

My hands were clammy and I was so anxious that we missed the paved road and I had to take them over the dirt road. My father didn't complain. He was still a good driver. Then, suddenly, the house was there, high in the meadow, its cedar exterior whitened by the deep green landscape. Slowly we drove up the bumpy gravel driveway. There was still a big pile of rubble near the garage. They didn't even notice.

"Now this is a house!" my father said as we got out of the car. He went over to the garage door and ran his hand along the new wood. Then they walked up the steps, and directly into the large space that was living and dining room and kitchen all in one.

"It's so big," my mother whispered. She looked around for him; he was standing near the dining room table in front of a bank of windows. He was looking south to the Connecticut hills. When he turned he could see the Catskills to the west. The house was on one of the highest spots in the Berkshires; from it we could see one gray barn. The rest was fields and hills, and beyond that, higher hills.

"It feels like the rim of the world," he murmured. We stood for a moment looking out.

"Where are Phil, and the kids?" my mother said.

"The car's gone. They probably went to get some tools for the garden," I said. She nodded. A few minutes later I called, "What kind of eggs?" But they didn't answer. They were wandering through the rooms like children in a candy house. They explored slowly, not even mentioning the little things that needed to be done. Those were details, fixable details. They were interested in the way the house was sited, the flow of space, the windows, the round stone fireplace that separated the kitchen from the living room, the storage space for the children's things.

And finally, again, the magnificent view. In the bright, almost summer sunshine they saw what they had not been able to see in the winter or in the rain: the shapes of the elms in leaf against the fields, the lushness of the timothy meadow, the white blooms of the apple trees along the meadow's east edge.

We ate; he first as always, then me, my mother last. I suspected they didn't eat at the same time even when they were alone.

"It's so homey already." My mother smiled as she sipped her coffee. Their eyes met for a second.

I sighed. The wood between the two banks of windows was stained.

"What's the matter?" he asked.

"The windows still leak." I pointed to the spot. "See, the wood is stained; it will have to be pulled out and replaced."

He arranged his hands into their peacemaking gesture. "Shah, shah, stop worrying, Laura, it's only money."

While my mother and I tidied up the kitchen my father stood by the window. "Where are they?" he kept saying.

"Herb, stop it. They'll be here. Phil is probably in a hardware store," my mother said. "Why don't you start unloading the car?" He nodded and started out, then she followed him. She was frowning. She had remembered all the breakable things she had wedged among the sheets and blankets and pillows.

"Grandma! Grandpa!" The children's noise preceded them. Then: "A beautiful house! Fantastic! So much bigger than I expected!" Exclamations floated toward me as I loaded the dishwasher and cleared the counter. Phil kissed me. He put some groceries down. "They really like it." He was unable to keep the surprise from his voice. We both laughed in relief.

"Now, let me look at you." Mother lined the children up as if she had been gone for a year instead of a month. I smiled as I listened. When my sisters and I were growing up it was her eye we feared: she could always spot a loose button or a crooked hem, a powdered-over pimple or hair that needed to be washed. My father never noticed. "Gorgeous," he said to us on our worst days. Now, with the grandchildren, she was just like him.

"Jessica's grown two inches, I swear it. And the little ones look marvelous. They're losing that baby look."

"Mom, I should hope so." I laughed. Mark was seven and Rachel four. As far as my parents were concerned they were all just born and I was still twenty-two. Sometimes when they saw my sisters and our husbands and our children all together I could see them asking themselves where all those extra people came from.

"They look like farm kids," my mother said as we watched them troop out to the garden in their overalls. It had rained over the Memorial Day weekend; we were late with the planting. The garden had been plowed but it needed more raking. From the way Phil walked I knew he felt pressed.

My mother saw it, too. "Go change and help him, Laura. I'll finish up here."

As we knelt in the garden the sunshine licked the backs of our necks. Now and then Mark and Rachel helped Jess and me plant; they dropped the seeds in the grooves we made, then lost interest and ran into the meadow to play in the high grass with Polly, our English spaniel. Once my father's shadow loomed long above; I felt like a child again, with him seeming so tall. "Phil's working too hard," he said.

Phil was at the other end of the graden, a bandanna around his head, sweat still pouring down his face.

"Phil's fine," I said. "He loves it."

By late afternoon we had planted several rows of lettuce, the beans, radishes, carrots, beets and zucchini. If the weather held we could do the rest in the morning.

The house was quiet. I could see that my mother had scrubbed the kitchen; somehow she could get things so much cleaner than I. Dad was sitting in the living room with two radios, one to each ear.

"Mother's resting," he told us.

"Why two radios?" Jess said. He looked up, startled.

"I can't get the news. My radio didn't work, so I borrowed yours and I still can't get anything." He looked helplessly at Phil and handed him one. In a few seconds Phil had found the station he wanted. He sat back, happy.

"Come, Jess, sit down and listen," he said. She smiled and shook her head. "I have to shower and change." She held up her hands. They were brown; she didn't like using gardening gloves. He shrugged.

"It's all the same anyway," Jess said. "Watergate. Watergate. What a mess!" I could hear myself in Jess's voice. Phil smiled at me over her head.

I washed my hands and started taking out food for supper. Soon Rachel came downstairs. She was in fresh clothes and Jess had done her hair in two tiny ponytails.

"Grandpa, can you play Scrabble with me?" she said.

"In a minute, just let me hear the end of the news."

"You go up and get the Scrabble set," I said. "You can play after supper."

As we were finishing dinner the conversation dwindled. The hay in the meadow swayed gently in the evening breeze. Rachel and Mark were playing cards quietly in the living room.

Suddenly my father's voice jarred us. "You know, Jess, Watergate isn't the worst thing that has happened to this country."

"There was the Civil War," Phil murmured, but it was ignored.

"No, kids, there are more important things than Watergate." Lately my father seemed to want to prove the country was healthy. We didn't agree with him and had been over it many times, but now, as I looked at his face, his features set for a political argument, I realized that he saw the country, even the world, in a very personal way — as something to give to his children and grandchildren. That was why he couldn't stop talking about it.

"You know, Jess, it's up to all of us to help continue the traditions of the country," my father said. "Where else in the world could the press, the radio, and television, even you and I criticize the President so openly? That's what this country is all about. Watergate is a scandal, but in the end it will be just a drop in the bucket." Jess was listening intently.

"It may turn out to be the whole bucket," Phil said quietly.

"She has such an intelligent face," my father said. Jess blushed; he didn't notice. He looked at me. "She'll be able to do anything she wants to when she grows up." He glanced at the younger children. "They all will." He turned again to Jess. "What are you going to be, Jess?"

She shrugged. "I don't know. Maybe a doctor," she said shyly. He raised his thick, gray eyebrows and shook his head up and down in approval.

Soon Mark and Jess and Phil pulled on their jackets.

"Where are they going?" my father said.

"To play baseball."

Rachel set up the Scrabble game. "We can play now, Grandpa," she said. But he had taken out the chessmen and was setting up that board. Next to him was a pile of chess problems he collected when he traveled.

"Grandpa!"

He didn't seem to hear her. My mother looked resigned as she wiped her hands on a dish towel. "Herb, Rachel is waiting."

"In a minute, I just want to work this out."

My mother sat down at the table. "Here, Grandma will play. Grandpa will come along later," she said.

My father didn't even realize he had disappointed the child. I watched him and wondered why. He caught me looking at him and held up the newspaper clippings. "Paris, Amsterdam, Brussels, and here's the best one — Jerusalem."

"Of course, the best one is always from Jerusalem," I teased him.

"Oh, go way." He shook his head. No one knew why these chess problems were so important to my father. It was hard for him to find anyone as good as he was at chess; occasionally he played with his older grandchildren, but he couldn't bring himself to let them win, so they got discouraged. These solitary chess games, I supposed, were a substitute for the games he used to play with his dearest friend, Max, who had died two years ago.

"Rachel, you'll be reading in no time," my mother was saying. Rachel rubbed her eyes.

"Come on, bunny, up to bed," I said.

"But Mark's still out."

"Mark's two years older than you, and he'll be in in a few minutes. Now march."

As we were reading a story, Mark and Jess came in.

"He's playing chess with himself again," Mark stage-whispered.

"Sh, sh, Mark. Leave him alone," Jess said.

Later, after the younger children were asleep, we sat reading. Phil had been able to get a concert on the radio; now they were playing Brahms. Next to me my father was going over the minutes of a board meeting at the temple. "A lot of talk and not much action," he muttered as he turned the pages.

"You could have refused to be on the Board," I said quietly. He stared at me as if I had lost my mind.

Suddenly Jess looked as if she were going to cry. "I hated it to end," she whispered. *Wuthering Heights* was on her lap.

"Oh, that's such a wonderful feeling." My mother smiled at her. "Come, darling, we'll make a cup of tea and I'll play you some gin." Jess's eyes brightened.

"How about a walk?" Phil stood up.

"Okay," I said. "How about you, Dad?"

"Why don't you two go alone?" my mother said quickly.

"Oh, Mom, don't be so silly. Come on, Dad, it'll do you good." He looked at his watch. It was ten o'clock; he had missed the news.

"How can I refuse if they put it that way?" he said to my mother.

The night was velvet on our faces. Clusters of fireflies helped light the way. Phil pointed out the constellations. "There's Regulus, Leo's back foot, and Cassiopeia, and the Little Dipper; the bright one up there is Vega and below that Cygnus. The sky is so big here! It's marvelous!" Phil hugged me to him as we walked.

"It's a beautiful spot, Phil, a beautiful house. I feel like a millionaire," my father said humbly, as if it were all Phil's doing.

"I hope you'll use it." My voice was bossier than I intended.

"Well, you'll be up for a few weeks" — my father started to count on his fingers — "and then Barbara is coming with her family, and then Erica and her kids will be here late in August."

"We won't be here continuously, and there's not just the summer. It should be gorgeous in the fall — the foliage, the weather," I said.

"But then there are the holidays, and after that I must go to Europe for business." He was hedging. Then he explained. "I wanted you kids to have the house. Just get yourself a little writing desk and close the door and you'll be all set, Laura. It will be so good for the kids, the air, a walk to the lake, the space. And your mother can come and stay a few weeks and read and walk."

"But, Dad, she wants to come with you," Phil said.

"Oh, I'll come on weekends and when you kids are here."

"But she wants to come with you, alone, for a while. It would be so good for you."

He spoke softly. "It's too quiet, too far from the rest of the world. That's why you kids like it, that's why your mother likes it, but it makes me itchy after a few days." We walked in silence for a few minutes. Phil had lingered behind with Polly.

It startled me to hear my father say this was too far from the rest of the world. For Phil and me these fields and forest and house were the real world — here we bent only to the rhythms of nature. But for him this was not enough. His world was a turmoil, a muddle of violence and corruption — that's why it needed such constant watching. And it was the watching that had interested him all his life, that would interest him till he died.

He put it differently. As he spoke the moonlight reflected in his brown eyes. "I've always loved the city, Laura. When I was a boy and my father took me to Vilna for a few days I was in all my glory. And when I got on that train to Berlin in nineteen twenty — my God, that was more than fifty years ago! — I felt freed."

"But, Dad, maybe you could learn to like it." I gestured toward the stars, the black fields, the scuffling sounds of the country night. "There's so much here — the garden, the lake, the music . . ."

He sighed. He could never make false promises, that I

knew. At last I could see that the house was simply part of his vision of himself and his family, as fixed as the stars in the constellations above. He had never intended to use the house, and for the rest of his life we would probably keep trying to convince him to enjoy it. The house was part of his legacy to us — perhaps to balance the chaos that was also our inheritance, whether we wanted it or not.

There was nothing left to say. I took his arm and slowly we walked back to the glowing house.

Company

WHEN ALL THE COUSINS IN MY FAMILY GOT TO-
gether, it was me they locked in the closet. Or used as the
patient when they played doctor. Or ran away and left me
counting alone in the yard, hiding my eyes, eagerly antici-
pating where I would look for them until, finally, I realized that they had once again abandoned me. Lips quiver-
ing, I would find my Aunt Beadie. "Don't cry, Mona,"
she'd say softly as she stroked my hair. And then she'd lift
single strands toward the light, trying to discover why my
hair didn't shine like the other cousins' hair.

"Children can be very cruel," she always said. "It will be
better when you're grown."

When I went to college — a good eastern girls' college,
on scholarship, of course — there was one blissful night
that first fall. About twenty girls in the scholarship dorm
(they had us all in one house just in case we tried to forget
we were poorer than the others) sat on the floor in my
room and listened to my records of Dvořák's chamber
music after the house meeting.

A few weeks later they elected me house president. Was
I proud! Even after I discovered that I was the janitor.

"She's president of her house at that fancy college they sent her to," Aunt Beadie bragged.

But even smart plain people need company. So if it isn't real company, if you're smart like I am, you make up company. There's no need to die for lack of someone to talk to.

You wouldn't believe what interesting friends I have. Once Virginia Woolf stepped into the car. It was a little awkward; she's very tall and I have a Datsun. But she managed, cape and all, and she hugged that beautiful mauve cape to herself and she stared at me with her marvelous sunken eyes and as we drove we talked. The usual, at first — the road, the fall colors (it was October), a bunch of geese flying south, the bearded philosophers in the sky (they looked like sheep to me, but why argue?). And then I said, "Virginia, with all your troubles, why didn't you ever visit Freud? Surely one of your friends could have gotten you an appointment." After all, sometimes the famous don't like to use their names — they prefer their friends. She sighed. I looked at her out of the corner of my eye, a little afraid I might have offended her. But she is, basically, despite the cape, very down-to-earth. "I was sure if I went to Freud I would never write again. The writing and the insanity were interlocked." She made it sound so simple that I didn't pursue it, though I'm sure she would have liked to be a better wife to Leonard.

Virginia comes back, though after that first time, never alone. Either with her sister Vanessa, or Leonard, or Bunny Garnett, once with Eliot. That was almost disastrous. He's so shy, and I was working so hard to get something, anything, out of his thin lips that I almost wrapped the car around a telephone pole.

At one time or another half of the people who are buried in Westminster Abbey have been in my car. And many who aren't buried there. I took a lot of English Lit at college, though I was a history major. My mother thought I would be another Mommsen. But who wants historians these days — not with the history we're making. So I took my master's in social work, finally succumbed to an afro (Aunt Beadie still says, feebly now — her shiny-haired kids put her in a home — "If only you had brushed it more as a child, Mona"), and I'm head of the social workers in one of those big New York hospitals. All day long I try to help people who have babies with birth defects, sisters with muscular dystrophy, brothers with heart trouble, parents with cancer. Not exactly the life I dreamed for myself. But at least there's money for the Datsun and weekends out of town. Every other weekend, there I am, on some parkway out of New York — to Vermont in the fall, to the Jersey shore in summer, or to Martha's Vineyard, Newport, Nantucket. In the winter it's the cities: Washington, Philadelphia, Boston — there are so many interesting places.

Kafka likes Philadelphia. He likes the quiet old Federal houses, and we have spent days in the Franklin Institute. Once I took him to Washington; he was fascinated by that wonderful pendulum they have in the Smithsonian. "I have finally seen time," he said when he saw it, but he won't go back. It was too noisy for him, the traffic frightened him, the crowds and lines depressed him. Even in Rock Creek Park, which is one of the most beautiful spots in the East, he seemed uncomfortable. "Look at her eyes!" I pointed to those incredible blue eyes of Mohini, the white tigress, stalking her cage. Kafka looked to please me, but he was miserable. "I could have written that lonely tigress," he murmured as we drove home. To divert him I started to talk about my job, but he said quickly, "Tell me something pleasant, Mona, please, just *happy* things."

When *Herzog* was published I had a definite sense of déjà vu. The people were different, but I had been doing it for years, and not just letters. Why write to someone if you can talk to him? Isn't that what the telephone ad says?

Today I am alone. Chekhov had to mulch his roses for winter, Henry James gets carsick on long trips, Napoleon had a stomachache, Bill Shakespeare had another date. Donne was free, but he's such dour company lately, I decided to pass. Occasionally I need to collect my thoughts a little. And it's pouring and there's a rainbow of leaves falling from the trees which, when they land, make the road slick. I need all my wits about me driving today. The slight element of danger in a slick road is exciting, though. Danger, no matter how slight, does make people feel adventurous, and with my hands on the wheel, I feel like those little boys who *vroom vroom* near the hospital all day long, imitating the ambulance call and the police whistle.

Vroom! Vroom! Now I'm in Vermont. I like crossing borders. New possibilities. So far I've been in thirty-six of the fifty states. I have a big wall map at home and I color in the states after I've been there. Sometimes I plan my vacations to see how many more states I can knock off. Once I drove my parents back to Florida just to color in more states. They didn't know that, of course. "You're such a good daughter, Mona," my mother crooned when we said good-bye. I am the only child, and they had high hopes for me, but this time I didn't get the usual lecture about finding a man and settling down and getting married like all your cousins are. Omission is sometimes bliss.

Jeesus Christ! I slam on the brake. I almost killed him! What an idiot to stand practically in the middle of the road wearing an orange jacket when everything else around is orange. He's young, probably in his early twenties, and wearing a pack. He throws it onto the back seat and then sits down beside me. He smells of wet wool and not too many baths recently.

"You're lucky you have all your toes," I say. Did I mention that he has a lovely dark beard? Fine and black and silky, and yes, almost shiny.

I almost never pick up hitchhikers because the car is usually occupied by my friends. But it is pouring and I practically killed him and, as I said before, I am alone. So why not? He doesn't look like the mugging type.

"I'm Louis," he says, "and you are very sweet to pick me up. It is raining very hard." He smiles a toothy smile, almost a caricature of a smile because he has such large, even teeth. He's glad to be in a dry place, that's clear.

"Are you from Paree?" He nods.

"Where are you going?"

"To Canada. I have a cousin north of Montreal. I'm going to stay there till Christmas and then I'll go home."

"Do you go to the university?"

"No, I am graduated, have graduated," he corrected himself. He speaks English slowly, but you can tell that he is getting the feel of the language.

"Where are you going?" He starts unfolding his map.

"Oh, I'm just out for a ride. No place in particular. Just out to see the leaves. But it rained instead."

"Yes." He smiles and gestures at the falling leaves with his skinny palms upward. "What is your name?"

"Mona."

"What do you do?" I can see he is making a guess in his head, and I wonder what I look like to him, but I can't exactly ask.

"Social work — in a big New York hospital. Help people face their lives." He nods.

"My cousin is an anesthetist in l'Hôpital de la Gare in Paris."

"Your cousin is a lot luckier than I," I say, but he goesn't get it.

Still, he's nice. And observant. And it's so good to smell an actual man in the car.

Maybe it was the smell that did it. Who knows? Who knows what makes people act the way I did? Because suddenly, after we had been riding for about half an hour, I wanted desperately to go to bed with him.

"Could you do me a favor?" I asked. His hand sought the window handle and he started opening it a little to get the fog off the windshield.

"Well, yes, that, too. But something else."

He raised his eyebrows.

"Could you go with me to a motel? Could you" — my palms were so sweaty they almost slipped off the wheel — "Could you sleep with me? It won't take long." I needn't have added that, because I could see, thank God, that he wasn't repelled. Just a little surprised. Well, maybe a lot surprised. So was I. But my surprise didn't make me take it back or try to make a joke of it or pretend I had had a moment of madness. The offer was still good, and as he paused before he answered, I could see that he was sizing me up.

Now although I'm not as good-looking as my cousin, who was freshman queen at Penn State, I'm not all that bad either. Plain, not really homely. I have sallow, slightly yellow skin that no amount of makeup can help, and going-gray dirty blond hair, but my figure is tidy and I do have a bust. A married doctor once lived with me off and on for about two years. I finally had to end that because the landlord was getting angry. He never wiped his feet when he came into the hall. It began to get under my skin, too. After he left the apartment I always had to vacuum. Where he found so much mud in New York I'll never know! The landlord was right; he had gotten to be boring anyhow.

Louis took his time. I didn't mind. There is something nice about having a real, actually substantial man looking at you. Kind of like Bishop Berkeley's question: Are you a woman if there is no one to see you as one? Well, Louis made me feel very womanly, and the more he looked the more I felt.

Finally he said, "Sure." That Americanese was perfect. I pulled into the nearest motel.

"My son would like to dry off and take a bath," I said to the clerk and pointed to Louis, who was still sitting in the car.

"You mean you're not staying for the night?"

"No, I'm sorry. We have to be on our way. My mother's

dying in Montreal. But my son had to change a flat tire and got soaked to the skin. With one member of the family dying I don't want to take any chances."

She gave me the room for half price.

Actually, I didn't feel like so much of a liar. As soon as the door closed, Louis asked if I wouldn't mind if he took a bath first. I said, "Of course not, take your time."

While Louis was in the bath I undressed slowly and got into bed naked and had an argument with Bill Shakespeare, who had gotten stood up and wanted to join me now.

"I already have a date," I told him in as harsh a whisper as I could muster, because Shakespeare is probably my favorite person in all of history.

Bill stroked his beard and looked at me kindly. "Enjoy it. You don't get a chance like this often," he said, and left quietly.

I lay there and looked around. It was the usual depressing motel room — avocado rug, green-flowered chair, and light green walls that reminded me of the hospital. Near the door was a large stain on the ceiling. I got out of bed and walked closer to it. The ceiling had been patched but it was just a matter of time before the leak would start again. When Louis came out of the bathroom with a towel wrapped around his waist I showed it to him. He smiled and went back into the bathroom and came out with a bucket that had obviously seen some use.

Louis's beard was not unlike Shakespeare's, and as we made love he whispered in French. Though I couldn't understand him, his tone was right. Everything would have been lovely if the leak hadn't begun about halfway through. *Plink, plonk. Plink, plonk.* The steady sound made me want to cry, but I tried not to show it. I guess I succeeded, because Louis looked very pleased with himself and promptly fell asleep in my arms. When he woke up we made love again, and although the water was still dripping I had gotten used to it. That time everything was better.

When I began to get dressed I noticed that a spider had begun to make a web in my underpants. My stomach was in a rage of hunger. I looked at my watch. We had been there four hours. But what better way to spend a rainy autumn afternoon in New England? We ate a little bread and jam from Louis's pack and then left.

"That must have been some bath," the clerk said when I returned the key. I could see in the mirror behind her that I no longer looked as if I had a dying mother. My sallow face was flushed.

"There's a leak in the ceiling of that room," I said brusquely, and ran to the car.

We had coffee and cereal and pancakes in a place up the road that served breakfast food all day. Louis didn't talk much; he kept looking at me with a puzzled expression.

"What's the matter?"

His voice was tinged with regret. "No one will believe me that this happened."

"Why do you have to tell anyone?" I said quietly. I hated to be laughed at over coffee cups.

"Because I'm not sure it will be real unless I tell anyone." He smiled his gorgeous smile. I nodded. That, at least, I understood.

"It's real if it's in your mind." I put my hand on his as he paused between pancakes. "Believe me. I know."

Back in the Datsun we rode peacefully. The weather was beginning to clear; there was going to be a sunset that would make everyone who saw it forget how much it had rained. From the vent on my side of the car I could feel the air getting crisper.

"Could you do me a favor?" I asked.

He spoke quickly: "I have to tell you, Mona, that my cousin in Montreal is a girl." I slowed down. All I had wanted was for him to open the window.

But he was uncomfortable. In Paris older women do live with younger men; maybe he thought I wanted to take him home. In a few minutes there was a picnic area on our side of the road, and I dropped him off.

Soon Shakespeare slid onto the seat next to me and we watched the sunset together in front of one of my favorite inns in all of New England. Then I had a long, leisurely dinner, and George Eliot and Henry Lewes stopped by for a nightcap, and I slept like a baby that night.

The first fifteen minutes at work Monday morning were filled with the usual resistance to the smell of the hospital. In short, I pressed my lips together while taking deep breaths through my nose to fight off nausea. By nine-twenty I felt as if I had been living there forever.

The waiting room to my office was filled. Criss-cross lines of suffering on the people's faces made me feel as if I were surrounded by a dozen pieces of human graph paper. And no matter what I did, arranged, or said, I couldn't help them. I was nothing more than Sisyphus in a white coat, a name tag, and a run beginning in my left stocking. Quickly I passed my puzzled secretary and all those resigned yet still hopeful pairs of eyes. I had to take a walk. If I didn't move my legs a little, I thought I would suffocate.

Emily Brontë joined me in the hall, and we closed our eyes and walked rapidly down the newly tiled corridors. We pretended we were striding along the moors. "Remember, Mona, how many died of tuberculosis then," she said. "And what good work they're doing here now."

"But it smells of death and dying. Why should good work smell of death?" I replied.

"The smell does defeat one," she admitted, and disappeared.

As I was going back to my office, my doctor friend stopped me. "Hi, Mona, how are you?" We're still friends. I don't believe in grudges. "Don't whine, Mona, and hold no grudges. They're dead ends," Aunt Beadie always said. She was right. Even history teaches you that.

"I'm fine," I said. "The foliage in Vermont was beautiful on Sunday after the rain. And I met a nice young man from Paris." Of course he didn't believe me. "And you?"

"The same." His mouth turned down a little at the corners; he expected some comfort, but I wasn't in the mood. I simply waited.

When he saw no sympathy forthcoming, he straightened his mouth briskly.

"Listen, Mona, you saved me a call. There are complicated problems in Room 201. The patient's wife had a heart attack over the weekend and is in Intensive Care. And in 117 there's a boy who was in a motorcycle accident. He'll be a vegetable. His parents are devastated. He was a Merit Scholar at Harvard," he added in a low, confidential voice. Obviously it was Harvard that impressed him. Whenever we talked, he never failed to remind me why I was relieved to see him leave my apartment for the last time.

"I know you'll see someone from both of those families today. Try to get back to me after four." He squeezed my elbow, either for Harvard or for old times, I suppose, and I headed back to the office.

It was a ghastly morning. One of the worst I've ever had. The stone gets heavier as we get older. By noon I was dripping wet — I perspire when I have to watch people cry. Before I went out for lunch I changed my bra and blouse and then picked up a sandwich and coffee and headed toward Central Park. It was a school holiday and they had closed the park to traffic, so as I ate I watched the bicyclers. They looked happy; I began to feel a little better.

Then Rilke came along and sat beside me. Now there's a man. I wished I had combed my hair. We chatted quietly and then, because the sun seemed to be having one last burst of energy before the fall really closed in, we moved to another bench and arranged ourselves so the sun could warm our faces. Saturday's storm had knocked so many of the leaves off the trees. I started to mourn the lost leaves, but then Rilke said, "They'll come back, Mona." He covered my hand with his. "It is so good not to be alone in autumn," he murmured.

After a bit a breeze came up, and although I protested, Rilke insisted on taking off his cape. Tenderly he spread it over my shoulders, and we sat there contentedly until it was time for me to get back to work.

Giving Blood

MY LITTLE GIRL HAS LEUKEMIA; SHE HAS HAD IT FOR over a year, and now she needs at least five pints of blood a day. Not the whole blood, just the platelets. Most of our relatives and friends have given at least a few times. But we need more. Now I have to go to strangers.

Alexander wanted to play with a new toy, but I was firm and dressed him and said, "Come on, Alexander, we're going for a walk. It's a beautiful day."

At the first house no one was home.

The next house was smaller, friendlier-looking. Hyacinths lined the front path. When she opened the door she smiled. "I know you," she said, "you moved in about a year ago. I've seen you walking along the road with the children."

I nodded. "My daughter is in the hospital." She was still smiling. "She needs blood. I was wondering if you could give blood. She has leukemia."

"Oh, I'm so sorry." Her face was filled with pity. My hopes rose. "But I can't give blood now," she said and stepped backward, her fingers touching her throat. "My brother-in-law had surgery a few months ago and I gave for him."

"But you could give platelets," I persisted. "She needs just the platelets and in an hour they can take them and return your blood to you. You rebuild the platelets."

"No. No. I told you, I just gave." Quickly she closed the door.

We passed a clump of Red Emperor tulips. Everyone makes such a fuss over them, I guess because of the color, but all I could see were splotches of blood. Blood in a garden, blood on the road being washed off by those powerful fire hoses, blood in the delivery room, covered with blood when they showed her to me. I was so surprised, I didn't think she'd look that messy. "Don't worry, dear, she's a beautiful baby, she just needs to be washed off and then you can hold her," the nurse said. Katharine we called her, thinking she would be Kate, but somehow it became Kathy.

Alexander started to cry. He had to go to the bathroom. I carried him to the door of the next house. She was still in her robe and her hair was disheveled.

"Can we use the bathroom?"

"Come in." We followed her down the hall.

"He was just trained."

"I remember those days," she said but didn't smile.

When we came out of the bathroom she said, "Are you new here?"

"No, we moved in a year ago." I took a quick breath, determined not to lose my chance. Her hand was on the doorknob.

"I didn't ring your bell just for Alexander. I was coming to ask if you could give blood. My little girl Kathy has leukemia." Her face didn't change.

"It takes only an hour."

Her eyes were vacant. Silence. Then, "I don't give for anyone but my family. It's a rule I made a long time ago." We were dismissed.

I look as though I'm collecting for a charity. That turns them off, I guess. People don't give the way they used to. My mother never refused anyone, she kept a jug of change in the kitchen and always gave a little. Money is easy, though, you just put your hand into the jug. Blood, that's another thing.

Long ago, when we were first married, Matt and I discussed it. Someone we knew was having open heart surgery. "Giving blood is a tremendously complicated matter for some people," he said then. "I once knew a man who said he could give it but never accept it. He was a Scot and afraid of getting Irish blood, or something like that." We had laughed.

And now — sometimes I don't even feel real.

What do you want? their eyes say.

Blood.

What d'ya want, *blood?*

Yes! I want to yell. There's nothing wrong with asking for it. It's okay. Legitimate. Even good. You all have it. Everyone! Flowing through your bodies. It's almost blue until it hits the air. A red ocean in my dreams, but it's blue, like the sea. Salt in the sea. Salt in your blood. They say that's proof of evolution.

The next house was gray with a yellow door. Colors seem to jump out at me these days.

"Yes?" she said.

"We came because we need . . ." I began.

"Come in, it's chilly." She smiled at Alexander. "How old is he?"

"Three."

"Our baby's a year. But she's down for a nap now." She pulled some toys from the bookcase. "What's your name?" She looked at Alexander.

1961932

"Alexander," he said.

"Here you go, Alexander." She handed him a Tonka truck.

"When did you move here?" she asked.

"A year ago, we're from the state of Washington."

"Oh, it's so lovely out there, why did you move?"

"We had to." I always try to sound casual but it never works. "Our little girl has leukemia and there's this marvelous doctor . . ." She couldn't say anything. She felt guilty — why me and not her, her eyes asked. I don't know.

"We need blood for her. She needs five pints a day and it's thirty dollars a pint, and what we don't get donated we have to pay for."

"Thirty dollars a pint?" She frowned. "What about the blood banks?"

"They don't have that quantity of blood. It's lasted so long."

"Of course I'll give. So will my husband. And I'll call some of my friends. I'm sure they'll help," she said casually. I wasn't so sure, but let her try. When Matt asked people at the college he thought everyone would help. Each night his face seemed grayer when he came home. He must have asked a hundred people. Thirty gave. His officemate said, "I'll do anything." When Matt asked him he turned green and said, "Oh, no, anything but that. I'm scared of needles."

She gave me a hot cup of coffee; it was good. She said her name was Lois.

"Where do you go to give?" she said.

"To the city. The hospital has a donor room."

"I just learned to drive and I've never driven in New York. Could you . . ." she hesitated.

"Of course I'll take you. I have to go tomorrow to give platelets. I'll pick you up at ten. Eat some breakfast at eight."

"I could try to drive."

"No, it's okay. I do it every day. It's easier for me to take my car. They give us stickers and there's a special parking lot for us."

I took Alexander's hand; she smiled as we left.

One. One out of three. It was only ten-thirty. For a second I thought of going home and pretending to be like everyone else — maybe I could finish the beds and do a wash and take down the bathroom curtain which looks so gray. But then that tightening at the back of my neck. No. I still had time before the baby-sitter came and I left for the hospital. Maybe I could get more.

Alexander's hand was suddenly heavy in mine. He started to shuffle.

"Let's sing, Alexander,"

> Row, row, row your boat,
> Gently down the stream,
> Merrily, merrily, merrily, merrily,
> Life is but a dream.

"No," he protested. "Kathy's way."

"Which way?"

"Kathy's way. Putt. Putt."

"Oh." I smiled, then we sang,

Row, row, row your boat,
Gently down the stream,
Putt, putt, putt, putt,
I'm a submarine."

"I want Kathy," he said. It was six weeks since he had seen her. He went into her bedroom every morning to see if she had come home. I picked him up and he held on to me very tightly all the way home.

The waiting room was empty. The irises had shriveled.

"I'll be right back," I said to Lois. They looked even worse in the wastebasket than in the vase. I went back and put them into the basket flowers down, hearing my grandmother's voice. "I won't have them in the garden, I can't stand to watch them die."

The nurse came into the waiting room.

"Hi, Miss O'Neill. This is Lois Slater, she's come to give blood for Kathy." Miss O'Neill smiled.

"Have you seen her yet?" she asked. I shook my head.

"Oh, she looks beautiful, sitting up, pleased as punch and fresh as a daisy today. Someone sent her a set of homemade dolls."

"We'll see her later." I went ahead of Lois because giving platelets takes longer. She looked a little frightened. She couldn't get another soul besides her husband to give blood, they all said they couldn't give for someone they didn't know. One woman told her she'd be lucky to get out of here alive.

The Markeseys were in the donor room. They give platelets together, they say it gives them a chance to talk, but it's too much for Matt and me. We tried it once; I couldn't watch him watch Kathy. Then she was well enough to come down and visit with us.

The Markeseys' boy Chris is still up, but from his color, well, who can tell, maybe he'll be lucky.

"How are you?" They were glad to see me. "Did you drive in?" They live near the hospital.

"Yes, it was a little windy along the river, but the forsythia is gorgeous."

"How's Alexander?" Chris is always interested in Alexander.

"Oh, he's fine. All trained and knows how to sing 'Row, row, row your boat.' " Chris grinned. Lois came in.

"Chris, this is Mrs. Slater, she's a friend of mine, and Marjorie and Tom Markesey, Lois Slater." Lois lay down and watched Chris help the other nurse tie up the packets of blood from his parents. The kids are amazing, so casual. Then Chris took the blood up to the lab. In a few minutes he was back.

"Don't know if I should let you in, Chris, after you cut me to the quick the other day." Miss O'Neill winked at Lois and me. "He doesn't like redheads any more, he prefers blondes."

"Blondes have more fun, Maggie."

"Traitor!"

A voice from the door boomed: "Well, well, if it isn't Christopher Columbus Markesey." It was Teddy. Brisk, matter-of-fact Teddy. It was always good to see him. He lay on the remaining table and beckoned Chris to him. Teddy usually says he doesn't care who gets his blood, but last week I heard him tell one of the nurses he'd like Chris to have it for a while.

"Is he — does he have a child?" Lois hesitated.

"Oh, no, Teddy's a construction worker on the job nearby, he comes every few days to give platelets," Miss O'Neill explained.

"Are there any others like Teddy?" Lois was amazed.

"Oh, about five, a group of friends — all young and in construction. They say they've no money, but lots of blood. They're all so happy-go-lucky, wonderful to have them around." Miss O'Neill held the orange juice for Lois. Lois looked at me and shook her head.

"Better stay there a while, my girl," Miss O'Neill cautioned her, then turned to me. "She has very low blood pressure, but since you're driving I let her give. We need whatever we can get, God knows," she said softly. I smiled gratefully and closed my eyes.

It's weird that the only rest I get these days is in this room, on a hard table, giving blood for my child. When I'm here I feel fine, it's where I should be. At home sleep never comes easily. Matt and I lie next to each other, pretending, yet Miss O'Neill told me that he fell asleep the other day with the needle in his arm.

"I'll go into the waiting room now, Anne," Lois said. I opened my eyes.

"I shouldn't be too long, they've already taken the blood up to the lab," I told her. I could have gone with her, but it was more comfortable to be with the Markeseys and Teddy.

"Now don't forget to concentrate on the math," Mr. Markesey said to Chris as they were leaving. Marjorie Markesey straightened Chris's sailor hat before she kissed him. All the kids are so sensitive about the hats and wigs under them. Having their hair fall out because of the drugs is the worst part of it for some of them. Now that she's in bed almost all the time Kathy doesn't bother with her hat, but she wears her wig when she isn't sleeping.

" 'Bye now, we'll see you," the Markeseys said. I waved. Chris saw them out, then asked Teddy, "Now what color?" He was coloring a large poster that was hanging on the far wall. He held up the magic markers.

"Orange."

"Great, Teddy, an orange alligator!"

I was finished. In exactly an hour. So what I tell people is true, but so few ever come back once they've given whole blood just to give the platelets. No time, they say.

Sometimes all I can see in my dreams is a huge pot, an ocean really, but contained in a pot — the stockpot of humanity — and the nurses and lab assistants dipping into it. No individuals, no asking, no packets. Just everyone's blood for anyone who needs it.

As we walked out of the waiting room I took Lois's arm. "Come on, I want you to meet Kathy. She's beautiful."

I could see that she didn't believe me, but when we stopped at the foot of Kathy's bed I saw that she understood. Kathy's wig is a poor imitation of her thick brown hair, but even in her wig she's lovely. Good bones, deep green eyes, such an intelligent expression. She was wearing new pajamas, purple, her favorite color. When she looked up her face was flushed.

"Look, Mommy, Jill sent them, aren't they great?" I bent to kiss her; she had a temperature, hard to tell how much.

"Yes they are, darling, and look at all the clothes." I turned to Lois. "Her best friend from Seattle. She sends something every few weeks, they're a wonderful family."

"Honey, this is Lois Slater, she lives up the road. She came to give blood."

"Oh, thank you. Do you have any children?"

"Yes, two boys and a girl. My younger boy is your age."

"Who does he have?" Kathy was so eager for any information about school. She had gone for a few months in the fall, but only for a couple of hours a day.

"Mrs. Blackfield."

"Oh, I got Miss Owens." Then her eyes brightened. "What's your son's name?"

"Peter."

"Could you ask Peter to tell Miss Owens I said hello?"

"Of course, Kathy, I'll be happy to."

"Grandma send the pajamas?" I poured some water into a glass and held it out for her to drink.

"Um, hm." She put the glass down and began to dress one of the dolls. Her schoolwork was piled at the foot of the bed. Each Friday I picked it up from school and the volunteers in the hospital corrected it. "Excellent," "Excellent," "very good," a smile face, the usual.

"It looks like you had a good morning."

"Yes," she said absently. Then she remembered something. She pulled a large piece of construction paper out of her night table. On it she had written, first in capital letters, then in lower-case, the word "quack." Underneath it said, "Quack begins with Q. Mother ducks teach their babies how to quack. That is how ducks speak. Mother ducks take good care of their babies." Below that was a drawing of a large white mother duck, and trailing behind her four small gray ducklings.

"That's great, Kathy." Lois handed me the drawing. Kathy had started this project the day after she went to the hospital. She was now on her second trip through the alphabet. Almost six weeks of drawings cover the walls in Alexander's room. The first Q says: "Q is for quiet. In the hospital it is too quiet at night." The drawing shows several kids asleep in identical beds. Now Kathy is more used to the hospital, and there are times when I know it is a relief for her to be here. If only she could see Alexander.

"Alexander will love it, darling. I can't wait to show it to him." But she was back to her dolls. We went out to the hall. Lois looked at the children's artwork: I talked to the nurse.

"Yes, a little bit of fever, nothing serious, a good night, today seems to be another good day."

I went back to kiss Kathy good-bye, just to feel her, to see her eyes bright, to know that blood was still moving through her. It was so discouraging at night not to be able to go in and check her, watch her sleep. It's such a unique pleasure — watching your child sleep. Okay, Anne, enough of that, I told myself. Lois looked tired, she had had it.

"Good-bye, puss. See you tomorrow." We waved.

No traffic and the sun was strong, the warmer weather was coming. Now the river was calm, the wind had subsided, everything sparkled. Except Lois. She was very pale.

"Are you all right?"

"Fine, just a little tired," she whispered. Then she leaned forward and put her head between her knees. I pulled over and grabbed a pillow from the back seat. After a few minutes she lay back on the pillow. Her hairline was ringed with sweat.

I handed her a Life Saver. "Here, this will help. You didn't tell me about your low blood pressure."

"I didn't realize it would matter, but I'll be all right. You know, Anne, I didn't believe you at first, but what an unusual child Kathy is! How pretty, and bright . . ." her voice trailed.

"I know. I have to admit it even if I am her mother. But all those kids are special. Some creepy doctor is writing a paper on how high the IQs of children with leukemia are. He's convinced there's something in their blood, the same thing that gives them leukemia gives them a high intelligence. No one agrees with him, but he thinks he has something and keeps questioning the parents." Lois looked at me incredulously. We were silent.

After a while she murmured. "I'm glad I gave." Then she slept.

I'm glad I gave. I gave. I gave. I gave, stop bothering me. I gave. When? Once in your life? Twice? Did you know you could give blood every six months, and they say it's good for you, it's a cleansing mechanism for your body? I could feel my hands tightening on the wheel. But anger is no help. I tried to relax.

After we paid the toll on the Henry Hudson Bridge Lois sighed. "Oh." Her voice was filled with disappointment.

"What's the matter?"

"I had the most wonderful dream, and it was so real. I guess it was really a fantasy. I was lying in the donor room and Chris took my blood up to the lab and then there was a call and we all went upstairs, and everyone took turns looking into a microscope. Then the doctor said, 'I think we've found it,' and the nurses touched my arm and I felt very happy . . ." She shrugged.

Tears filled her eyes. She wanted me to comfort her, but what could I say? Silently I pulled up to her house.

"Won't you come in, Anne? I'll make some coffee."
Lois's eyes told me she wanted us to share the pain we both
felt. How could I disappoint her? She, a stranger, who had
given blood for my child. But it was too much to ask. My
nerves were ragged; I was beginning to get angry.

"I'm sorry, Lois, I have to get home." I avoided her eyes,
hating myself. As I pulled the car out of the driveway I
waved.

"Thanks."

"What?" She frowned.

"Thanks for giving blood," I called.

The next morning was another magnificent day. We
were out at nine. The tight magnolia buds reminded me of
hungry infants' fists. At the bottom of our driveway some
daffodils had bloomed in the night. Alexander pushed his
new toy lawnmower as we walked down another road
looking for blood.

Lost

AFTER MY HUSBAND, HENRY, HAD BEEN GONE FOR AL-
most a year I decided to get a job. Not that I needed it;
Henry left me comfortable, and I did feel guilty with unemployment on the rise, but I didn't know what else to do.

There are alternatives to a job, I know. I've tried them.
For years I went to the New School — three, sometimes
four, times a week. It used to be the family joke: Henry's
joke. "Well, what pearls did you learn today?" he would
say as he flicked open his napkin at dinner. But once he
was no longer there to talk to about the courses, I stopped
going. It's like eating. When I am alone I scarcely care
what I eat.

I tried volunteer work in a hospital. That depressed me.
Henry was a brave man when he was dying; you can't
imagine how many moan and groan. No pride at all.

It was my friend Molly who suggested I volunteer at the
local school. "Remedial reading or math drill — it's right
up your alley, Alma," she said one day, so I walked over to
the elementary school, the same elementary school Paul
and Barbara had gone to. I stood at the fence of the large
playground and watched the children. They were all so

beautiful. I started to go to see the principal — not the same one my children had, of course, but a nice man I know by sight. I never got there; for some crazy reason I began to cry.

"You need something less personal," Molly said when I told her about it. We were meandering through the stores on a rainy afternoon. She had a thousand things to do, but she didn't want me to be alone. I was looking for a blouse for my daughter Barbara's birthday. A saleslady helped me find exactly what I had in mind. Seeing her smile and hearing the voices around me, I suddenly felt better. I dropped Molly off and went home to find something to wear. Then I called a man Henry had known in the management at the local branch of Lord & Taylor. I told him I would like to work at the store. He called me back to say I had an appointment with the Personnel Department the following week.

Wouldn't it be wonderful not to be home when Paul and Barbara called every morning! It had got to be such a chore for them, especially for Paul, who is a psychiatrist and busy enough with his patients' problems. On the phone he always sounded distracted.

"What department would you like to work in, Mrs. Fulton?" Mr. Moran said. He was director of personnel, but if you saw him on the street you'd think he was still in high school.

"I don't know, it doesn't matter, anywhere . . ."

"Well, let's see." He ran his hand through his curly, reddish hair." Toys?"

I shook my head. They're so expensive, and kids don't play with them much anyway.

"Women's clothes?"

I could feel my face crumple.

"Now, Mrs. Fulton, don't get discouraged. We'll find something you feel right about. Something that requires good taste; you're obviously a woman who has good taste."

He must have had to take a lot of psychology in college. I tried to smile.

"I like your scarf, I really do," he said. He turned around and took a file out of a cabinet. His eyes scanned a long page. "How about housewares?"

I gathered my courage. "Is there . . . are there any openings in the men's department?" I asked.

He hesitated for a second. "That's it," he said, and he made a few notes on a pad. Although he said it would be a week before I heard officially by mail, I knew I had the job.

On my way out, I wandered through the men's department. Its dark brown and blue walls were soothing. Soft lights shimmered on the glass cases. I remembered how, on hot days, my mother drew the shades in her room, and my sister and I rested on my parents' twin beds. Sunlight sneaked in through the cracks and jumped back and forth on the mirrors and perfume bottles and cut-glass lamps.

I walked slowly through the department. I stopped in front of the Liberty print ties and tried to recall Henry's suits (they still hung on his side of the walk-in closet) . I left quickly.

Instead of going home, I took the next train to New York and stood in line for forty-five minutes to see *Murder on the Orient Express.* I hadn't been to a movie in the daytime since my kids were small. And Henry hated standing in lines. After the movie I found a Chinese restaurant I had read about in the *New York Times*. Chinese restaurants like this one are so noisy that you feel you belong to a big family. On the train home, I composed a letter to Craig Claiborne in my head, and for the next few days I went through my closets to find some decent spring and summer clothes. The summer would be a good time to start working — things are slower and it would give me a chance to get used to the routine. I had worked only once before. When I married Henry, I was a secretary to an executive in a small milk company.

"A saleslady?" Barbara said.

"What's wrong with a saleslady?"

A long pause. "How about more courses, Mother?"

"There's not much left that I want to take."

Barbara laughed a little nervously. Another pause. "Well," she said finally, "now I'll have to buy everyone's clothes at Lord & Taylor's."

Paul was worried. "How can you stand on your feet all day?" he said.

"Is it dangerous?"

"No, it's not dangerous. You have no history of varicosity or circulatory problems. But it's going to be damned uncomfortable!" That was how he sounded when I used to want to discuss Erikson or Jung with him — when I was going to the New School.

"I'll change my shoes often," I promised.

Three weeks later, my feet still felt fine. I had learned to change my shoes every couple of hours and was wearing sandals with a little heel. No space shoes for me. I could tell that I was getting along all right from the way people looked at me. I don't like to make much of this but I'm known as a pretty woman for my age. If I have a flaw it's that I'm vain. For almost a whole year after Henry passed away I didn't look in mirrors at all; now I was starting to see my reflection again.

The days passed quickly because I played a continual game in my head. When a customer approached I asked myself, "Will she buy?" Then, "How much?" Then, "What?" Most of my customers were women. Some spent more than they could afford because they were not shopping for themselves. I liked them. A lot were young, well dressed, and a little rushed; others shopped leisurely behind strollers or carriages. Waiting on them, I thought about some of my courses: Is the Family Obsolete? The Women's Movement and the Destruction of the Nuclear Family.

"Theory isn't life," Henry used to say.

I tried to avoid the older customers. So many complained about their husbands: he likes cotton and there's only permanent press; he won't wear French cuffs, he'll only wear French cuffs; he wants to know why they don't make summer pajamas with strings instead of elastic. Once I started to go see Mr. Moran about changing departments, then decided to give it another day. The next morning was slow. I lingered in the corners of the department and gathered my wits a little. After lunch a charming woman came in to buy clothes for her son, who was getting married. We had such a good time. "I remember doing this for my Paul almost twenty years ago," I told her.

One evening Barbara called. "Are you free for lunch tomorrow?" she said, and suggested we meet at the store's terrace restaurant. Her voice was cheerful. She was getting more rest now that the kids were at camp. I was so pleased, especially when she said that Marge, Paul's wife, would join us. It wasn't often I had both girls to myself.

I wore a new brown and white print I had bought in Better Dresses to work next morning. "Don't you look pretty, Alma!" people in the department said.

"Barbara's coming for lunch. With Marge." There was no need to explain. Everyone I worked with knew about my family.

At lunch, Marge looked tired. She should have sent her kids to camp like Barbara. I had tried to persuade her that two teenagers on her hands all summer was too much, but she and Paul were against it. Not because of the money, though. I was sure it wasn't that.

Whenever people passed our table they smiled, and I smiled a good deal myself. I was so happy to see Marge and Barbara both relaxing a little that at first I didn't notice the change in Barbara's voice over dessert.

"We didn't want to tell you until you felt stronger," she was saying.

I looked at Marge; she avoided my eyes. My ears pounded, I strained to listen.

". . . and he's having trouble walking," Barbara said. I became afraid. "Who, what are you talking about?" I said.

"Paul," Barbara said. She reached over and put her hand on mine. "Paul has multiple sclerosis. We found out shortly after Dad died." Her voice was quiet, controlled.

Marge seemed mute. Her lower lip trembled, she was

nodding like one of those dolls that do everything in the toy department, but she didn't speak. I knew how she felt. There was nothing to say.

I simply nodded and drank the rest of my coffee and got out my wallet to take care of the tip.

The girls wanted to take me home so I could rest, but I would have died in that silent house so I went back to work and pretended that nothing had happened. People still remarked, "What a pretty dress!" I still smiled and waited on my customers.

I saw the sweater during my three o'clock break and knew I had to have it for Paul. It was in the stockroom. A yellow cashmere V-necked slipover — a true yellow, not flecked with dark specks the way light-colored cashmere used to be. Holding it was like holding the sun in your hands.

"They're just in from Scotland, Mrs. Fulton. Gorgeous, aren't they?" the buyer said. He is a young man and insists on calling me Mrs. He and I went out on the floor and chose a good spot to display the sweaters. We decided on my countertop. They came in several colors, but the yellow was the best. It would be perfect with Paul's dark hair and eyes.

There were two sweaters in Paul's size. I watched carefully as people admired the display, even touched the fine wool, but it was too hot to buy a cashmere sweater. "I'm looking for tennis shirts and they're showing cashmere sweaters," one young woman muttered to her friend as they swept through the department.

About half an hour before closing time I looked at the

sweater again. It was marked sixty dollars. With the personnel discount, closer to fifty. I could certainly afford that. I started to reach under the counter for my book, then I was opening the bag I keep my extra shoes in and stuffing the sweater into it. I looked around; no one was in sight.

I zipped the bag shut and walked with it toward the package room where they keep the lockers and time clock. "Leaving early, Alma?" someone said. It was Noreen.

"Yes, I have a headache. Do you need me for anything?"

"No, go along. You've had a big day." Noreen has no children and is awed by people who do.

I told myself I would mark it in my book tomorrow. If anyone asked why I took it today I would say it seemed easiest, since I was going to Paul's for dinner. But even then I think I knew I wanted to steal that sweater. By the time I got to the car, I had dismissed the idea of paying for it.

The car was cool. I always park under some tall trees at the far end of the lot. I sat down in the front seat. I put my head back. My hands crept to the shoe bag and pulled out the sweater. They held the cashmere up to my face and stroked my cheeks and neck with it. I began to cry. But luckily the tears sat on top of the wool. Seeing them there, little drops of salt water on the new sweater, I came to my senses and wiped them off.

"A cashmere sweater in July?" Paul said. He looked amused. He was sitting with his legs up on the ottoman in his den. As he held the sweater up to him I wondered how I could have been so unobservant. Last fall he had stopped playing tennis, said he was too busy. He and Marge had

scarcely gone out all winter. "Records are better than concerts," he had told me. He looked older, tired. Three
weeks ago he'd said he had a bum leg, and all last weekend
he hadn't left his chair.

"The nights are cool," I said, apologizing not so much
for the gift as for my stupidity.

"It's beautiful, Paul," Marge said.

Leave him be, I wanted to tell her. He has a right to be
annoyed with such a dumb mother. Instead, I sat with my
hands folded in my lap.

"Now, Mom, try not to get too upset," Paul said. "Multiple sclerosis often progresses very slowly." (He was making that part up, I think; the article in the encyclopedia
that I read when I stopped at home mentioned nothing
about slow progression.)

Later, when I was leaving, Paul reached out to take my
hand. "And there are often plateaus, even remissions. I can
still practice. What if I were a pediatrician?" Paul grinned
at me. I wanted to hug him, but I was afraid of hurting
him. I plucked a little at his arm. He pulled my head
toward his. "I really like the sweater, Mom," he said.

When he was little he always looked forward to his
birthday more than Barbara did. Once in a while Henry
and I would get him something that was absolutely wrong.
One year it was a printing press instead of more trains, a
few years later it was a fancy telescope when he had wanted
a new bike. Seeing our dismay, he would say, "I really like
it, I really do," over and over again.

The next day they discovered the sweater was gone. I
helped look for it. After two hours of searching the buyer
said, "I was foolish to put them out on a counter. It was

my own fault." Quietly we folded the sweaters and put them into a glass case. I felt completely detached from what was happening. It was eerie.

A week went by. At work I was so busy I scarcely had time to think. When I got home I ate something, watched a little television, and went to bed early. The only people I spoke to besides the kids were Molly and my insurance broker. On Friday night I went to Paul's for dinner. Barbara and her husband, Bruce, were there. When it was time to eat, Paul tried to get up out of the easy chair alone. He began to sweat at the temples and Marge helped him stand. Once he was upright he seemed fine, although he held onto Marge's arm for the first few steps. No one said anything. Barbara and Bruce turned to look at the show of Starfire phlox in the garden.

My daughter, Barbara, puzzled me. We had always been close. Now when she called and said, "How are you, Mother?" I wanted to answer "I'm desperate," but she would never let me. She just chatted on and on about her kids and Bruce. She made me feel that discussing Paul or Marge would be betraying them.

By lunchtime on Monday morning I had a new pair of men's cotton pima pajamas in my shoe bag and a brown calf wallet. No one in the department knew about Paul. Molly knew before the kids told me, but I couldn't see hanging my troubles out on the line for my new friends. It's bad enough to be a widow. I showed the pajamas to Marge after work. "They were putting these on special purchase, so I picked up a pair for Paul," I said.

A few days later, when I took over the wallet, I could see that Marge was upset. "I don't like you to be spending all that money," she said firmly.

The strangest part was that I didn't feel guilty. It was as if some other woman had stolen the things and given them to me. That night I pulled out all the psychology textbooks I had bought over the years. As my hands turned the pages I looked at them. The veins were more prominent, a few of the knuckles had thickened, but otherwise they were the same hands that had loved Henry and cared for Paul and Barbara and cooked thousands, maybe a million, meals. How could they have learned to steal? And so quickly?

Before everyone knew it, it was Labor Day weekend, and I was going to a barbecue at Paul's. When I arrived Barbara's car was in the driveway. The house hummed with children's laughter. Yet a chilly breeze blew across the asters and marigolds along the front walk. The sun was low, summer was dying.

I carried a large bowl of potato salad I had made into the kitchen. Something glistened in the breakfast room. In the corner was a shiny wheelchair. It reminded me of the Bilt-Rite baby carriage we had bought when Paul was born. Much too expensive and well made for someone who planned to have only two children, but that was what people had then and when he saw how much I wanted it Henry had indulged me.

"He doesn't need it yet, but the doctor suggested we have it in the house," Marge said. She put her arm around me. I should have let her take me in her arms right then and there and I should have cried as I wanted to, but somehow I couldn't. Everyone else — Barbara, Bruce, Paul himself, even the kids — seemed so brave that I felt I had to be brave, too.

Still, at dinner I couldn't believe how cheerful they were. Everyone was talking and laughing. Anger welled up in me. As I ate, tears rose to my eyes, but no one noticed. Barbara's kids were describing a big show they had put on at camp.

The next Saturday I went to the doctor, fully intending to tell him everything, but when I got there I lost my nerve. I said I had been bothered by chest pains, then talked a little about Paul — how calm he and Marge and the children were.

"MS victims often seem to be optimistic," he said. "Even euphoric. Some doctors think it goes with the disease. And you know, Alma, there are remissions, sometimes long remissions. And he can work and they are doing research . . ." I shook my head and he stopped. After I was dressed he gave me a prescription for a tranquillizer. I had it filled, then threw the bottle out a few weeks later.

Paul was in the wheelchair for a good part of October. When he wheeled himself in to dinner he would grab the edge of the table with one hand, put his arm around Marge or Vivie, and hoist himself into the dining room chair. Each time, I stood quietly at my place and watched as his legs dangled in the second before he sat.

During October I stole a ring for Marge, a dress for Vivie, and a canvas suitcase for Barbara's son, Steven. I simply picked up the suitcase and walked through the store with it.

"Going on a trip, Alma?" Noreen asked.

I smiled in reply.

In the middle of November there was a notice on the employees' bulletin board about shoplifting. From the wording it was clear that the employees were suspect. For three days I imagined that people were watching me. I was frightened to think I might lose my job. I wouldn't know what to do with myself.

I called Molly the third night, determined to confess. But when I heard that kind, reasonable voice I couldn't bring myself to say anything. I hung up. I took a piece of paper and wrote on it in black magic marker *You must stop stealing!*, then tore it into tiny pieces and threw them down the toilet.

That seemed to help. But a few nights later I had a nightmare: I was lost and sliding on some smooth shiny metal surface in the middle of nowhere. Just as I was about to fall someone caught me. Then I was locked in a shower stall in the rose-pink bathroom of my childhood. A harsh-voiced person handed me a couple of Ritz crackers over the top of the door.

The next morning I put a few items I had stolen and not yet given away into a grocery bag. On my way to work I dropped the bag in the Goodwill box in the village. When I got to the store there was a message in my box asking me to see Mr. Moran. I broke into a sweat, wondering what I could say when he accused me. But he smiled when I came in, and left his door open. "You're one of our best employees, Mrs. Fulton," he said. "I knew you would be when I interviewed you. And I thought you should know that we're giving you more than the customary Christmas bonus on December first and you will be promoted to assistant manager of the men's department, starting January." Luckily his phone rang and I could escape without having to say more than a dry "Thank you."

The following Sunday we went out to eat. Miraculously Paul didn't need the wheelchair now. The only indication of his illness was the cane he carried and the deeper lines around his eyes. We walked very slowly to the restaurant; Marge and the kids went ahead. Someone waved as we entered. "Too much tennis?" he called. Paul chuckled deep in his throat. Henry's laugh. I felt calm for the first time in months.

At the table, after we had ordered, Marge said, "What's new at the store, Mom?"

"There was a notice on the employees' bulletin board a few weeks ago about shoplifting. It's getting out of hand, and apparently employees do it, too." My voice was wary, but I had surprised myself and was talking about it.

I expected them to be shocked, but Vivie nodded. "A lot of kids I know steal, but mostly from five-and-dimes. They say it's fun. One of them took so many things he had to put some back on the shelf. That's when the shopkeeper caught him."

"One teacher had so much gum stolen from her desk that she finally wrote on the board: 'Buy your own gum!' " Jeff added.

"Why would anyone steal gum?" Marge asked Paul. Then Marge looked at me. Her eyes were thoughtful, and for a moment I thought maybe she knew why I had mentioned the shoplifting. But when she spoke, her voice sounded as if it were being filtered through water. "I once knew a wonderful man who stole something," she said quietly. "His wife was in love with someone else — in this case another woman — and one night, when he was working late, he took a huge *Webster's International Diction-*

ary from his office. He lugged it downstairs to the lobby of the building and started to walk home. From midtown to his apartment in the East Sixties. He finally took a cab."

Our food came. As the waiter was placing it in front of us I thought about that poor crazy man. Before I knew it, tears were dribbling down my cheeks.

"Here, Mom," Marge said, and she helped me to the ladies' room. She didn't ask me to explain, and I was grateful. I wouldn't have known what to say. I didn't even know why I was crying.

"Things pile up on all of us," she said softly. I nodded. Later, I told them about my raise and promotion.

December. I bought all my Christmas presents early and didn't put a thing in my shoebag all month. It snowed a lot before the holiday, so after Christmas dinner the children went out to play. Paul and I watched them from the sun room. Marge and Barbara and Bruce had insisted I relax while they cleaned up. I did my needlepoint and Paul read. The cane was propped against his chair. After a bit he asked me to put on some Beethoven Quartets, and he closed his book and leaned back and listened. I thought of the first summer he was home from college, when he had played Beethoven's Ninth every single night. Though the wheelchair was not in sight, I knew it lurked in some corner of the house. Sure enough, by the end of January Paul was in it again.

"Don't be upset, Mother," he greeted me. "This sometimes happens with cold weather. "Please don't be upset." I was so proud of myself that I didn't cry.

When the merchandise for the midwinter sales was put

out, I knew it was hopeless. I could feel my hands starting to move toward the shoe bag. My head began to spin.

I went to Mr. Moran. "I'd like to take a leave of absence — for reasons of health," I said.

His face fell. "Mrs. Fulton, I can give you a month's vacation," he said, "maybe even a little more — only two weeks paid, of course, the rest at your own expense. But we can't give you a leave unless you've been here a year."

I thought for a moment. Maybe six weeks would do it. Then I shook my head. "No, I'll need more time. My son is ill; he's a psychiatrist, but he's sick anyway . . ." I gestured helplessly.

Mr. Moran walked me back to the department, saying, "Don't worry, Mrs. Fulton, whenever you want to come back, as long as I'm here you'll have a job. And you can start at the same salary as you have now, I'll make sure of that." He shook my hand very hard.

I left the store that afternoon. People from the department were puzzled. Noreen tried to insist on making a date for a farewell lunch. I said no. She called for weeks. "Please come see us," she urged. I was so pleased to hear from her but I could barely drive past the store; I was afraid I would pull into my parking spot and go to Mr. Moran and ask for my old job.

Now I'm back at the New School. I take the train into the city three times a week for my courses: You and Your Genes, The History of China, The Quest for Happiness. Barbara is relieved, and so is Paul, I guess. He didn't say much when I told him I was leaving the store. Only Marge was concerned.

"It's been so good for you. Maybe you can go back when you feel better. At least part-time," she said, and kissed me.

The other people in my classes aren't terribly exciting, but once a week, on Wednesday, all the widows go out for dinner. They think I lost my job. One said gently, "So many people have been let go, Alma." I couldn't tell her the truth, so I nodded. And Molly and my other old friends call more often now that I'm not working. Whenever we do things together, Molly tells me I'm managing very well.

I didn't know you could miss a place as much as I miss the store. The people. Feeling part of the world. Maybe someday I can go back. But I've already paid for the semester, and some of the reading is interesting. Besides, for now, it's safer here.

part
two

In the
German Bookstore

THE WILDEST THINGS SEEMED POSSIBLE WHEN YOU were young. Herschel had thought he would read all the books in the world.

What had happened? He was seventy-four years old. His health was good. So was his business. He made the 7:07 into New York in the morning and the 5:33 home in the evening — five days a week. He no longer went on the road, but twice a year he and his wife, Frieda, went to Europe on buying trips. All three daughters were married, two sons-in-law in the business. Eight grandchildren. "That's a day's work," someone said recently. Herschel and Frieda had smiled proudly.

In whatever spare time he had Herschel read. His father had been a rabbi so he was fluent in Hebrew and German as well as English and Russian. Most of all he loved the English poets: Milton, Browning, Oscar Wilde. "Ah, that a man's reach should exceed his grasp, / Or what's a heaven for?" "Stone walls do not a prison make," he used to say so often that his daughters had been astonished when they realized the phrases were lines of poetry. He was the only person they knew who read the eleventh edition of the Encyclopedia Britannica for pleasure. Just recently he had looked up Madame Blavatsky and the theosophist movement because his well-educated children had been arguing about the meaning of anthroposophism.

People praised him for his wide range of knowledge, for his successful business, for his family, for his interest in politics, for his generous, forgiving nature.

"Too forgiving," one friend said when Herschel announced his plans to go to Germany for the first time in thirty years for the Frankfurt Fair. Even Frieda was taken aback.

"How could you, of all people, go there?" she asked him. Herschel's older brother had been killed with his wife and young children by the Nazis. Herschel shrugged. He had heard from enough of his friends and acquaintances how they would never set foot on German soil.

"We have to learn to forget, even to forgive, as hard as it is. No one can hold a grudge forever," Herschel said quietly. From his tone Frieda knew that the subject was closed; they went to Frankfurt that spring.

The following fall, soon after the Jewish New Year, Frieda began nagging Herschel about his desk. It was old, scratched, the drawers stuck, and when they moved into the apartment several years ago the movers had broken a back leg. Crammed with papers of doubtful value, the desk was virtually unusable. When Herschel brought work home he spread it out on the dining room table. One rainy Sunday Frieda gave the ultimatum. She had found a lovely Hepplewhite desk at the local cabinetmaker's and it was to be delivered next week. "If you want anything from your old desk, you'd better go through it now," she said severely and handed him a few cartons. "If not, out." She swept the air around her toward the door. "The entire thing is going out. The superintendent's son is eight years old and has been asking for a desk."

Not a day for choices, that was clear. Herschel took his FM radio and closed the door to the combined study–spare room where his desk stood between two large windows. Gusts of wind blew up stray pieces of paper from the street below and a few chickadees complained of the cold, but soon he ceased to notice anything. Slowly he went through old office mail, Father's Day cards, notes to himself on what to read, frayed book reviews. Then he found the manila envelope. In it, along with the yellowing immigration papers and vaccination card, were two sepia photographs. One was of a small, frightened-looking boy wearing a hat far too big for him. He was holding a bunch of newspapers in his arms. He stood very straight in front of a wooden house whose symmetrical windows had scalloped white frames. Another person stood a few feet away from the boy — a handsome uniformed man in his thirties. In the second photograph the boy was ankle deep in snow; he wore high boots, a thick dark coat and a wool hat pulled down over his ears. He stood proudly in front of a more modest house, a wooden cabin, really. Again the soldier was nearby, this time talking to an older man on the front steps of the house. Herschel smiled and put the photographs into his billfold and finished cleaning his desk. Frieda was right. What he wanted to save filled only about a third of one carton. He didn't mention the photographs to his wife. He wanted to tell the story first to one of his children.

Next weekend they went to Laura's house for dinner.

After the meal everyone went in different directions. Only Laura, his eldest daughter, and Herschel lingered at the table over coffee. They passed various sections of the Sunday paper back and forth to each other, not talking much. After a while Herschel pulled out his billfold and pushed the photographs toward Laura.

"What were you doing?" she asked.

"Working in the German bookstore. I found them last week when Mother insisted I clean my desk. I had almost forgotten about that bookstore, or at least that it had happened to me. At my age it seems incredible that that small boy is me," he said with a smile, then took a breath and began.

"It was nineteen fifteen. I was thirteen and a half years old. The German army was establishing an eastern front and we had heard that they were coming to the Beresina River, which was about twenty kilometers east of Olshan, our town. People were packing up and running away because they knew the Germans were going to use Olshan for their headquarters. Two roads ran through Olshan — it was a good-sized town, not a village. We had packed our linens and mattresses and a few dishes and some pillows into large cartons and were waiting for the farmers my father had hired to come with their wagons and take us to Minsk. From there we planned to take a train to Kharkov, where we had family. We had packed the books and furniture and put them into the small brick building that stood behind our larger wood house. We knew the Germans would confiscate the wood house as it was one of the biggest houses in town, and my father hoped his books would be safer from looting or fire in the outbuilding.

"My mother woke us early and we dressed and had breakfast, then packed the breakfast dishes. Ten of us — my parents, my mother's father and seven children. The youngest was still an infant and we took turns holding him that day — as if we were afraid that if we put him down we would forget him. We waited for the farmers on the terrace in front of the house. Finally we could see them jogging along in their cart. Behind them was a dark cloud that seemed to be moving along the ground. Before long we realized it was the Russian army retreating. Cannon and horse-drawn wagons carrying the officers and supplies crawled along the main road. On the secondary road that went through the forest the infantry plodded through the mud. The retreating army meant that the Germans were closer than we had thought. When the farmers reached us they announced that they were not going anywhere. If they attempted to take us to Minsk in the midst of a retreating army, surely they and we would be killed.

" 'They are right,' a Russian colonel told my father as he stopped in front of our house. 'You cannot get mixed up with a retreating army. If you stay you will be safe, the Germans will not hurt you.'

"So we stayed in Olshan. We unpacked our bundles and crowded into the back rooms of the house because the Russian colonel needed the front rooms for his headquarters during the retreat. Quickly the soldiers set up radios and telephones, and we spent almost two weeks watching the army pass through the town. First the infantry, then the Cossacks on their horses. Since it was still fall, they wore their big black capes with the cloth on the outside and the fur on the inside. Huge black capes and fur hats. They carried spears with sharp metal tips." Herschel stopped for a moment, astonished at the shiver of excitement he felt down his spine. Always, when he saw those Cossacks, he had felt fear, but fear mixed with awe and, yes, admiration. To look that strong! To ride those magnificent horses! Secretly he had wished to be one of them, but his wish had filled him with shame. Even now he couldn't share it.

"They were the same Cossacks who used to charge through the town on guerrilla raids before the war and then they looted, but now they were with the army and on better behavior. Only one Cossack tried to give us trouble. Somehow he had found his way into the brick house and tried to pry open one of the cartons of books with his spear, but my grandfather ran after him. My grandfather had been to America in nineteen five and knew a little English, so he grabbed a shepherd's staff and ran after the Cossack, shouting in English, 'Get out of here, you son of a bitch!' and the Cossack fled.

"Then the Russian army was gone and on Succoth, the harvest festival, the Germans came. They, too, decided to use our house for their headquarters. The officer in charge of setting up the camp was named Lieutenant Kline. I don't think he cared much for Jews but he respected learning. When he discovered that my father was a rabbi and saw all the books we had begun to unpack he was very decent to us. After a few weeks he realized how uncomfortable we were, crowded into the two back rooms of the house, and he moved his headquarters to the house next door and that family, the Boyarskys, came to live with us. A few houses down the road Kline set up the bookstore.

"This was a real bookstore, not a commissary. It had only books and newspapers and supplied the soldiers when they were rotated out of the trenches on the border along the Beresina River. The soldiers came back to Olshan for a week or two at a time and they needed something to do, so there were huge shipments of books from Germany, hundreds of books, and all the newspapers from Germany and Poland, too.

"The man who ran the bookstore was named Feldblum. He was older than the rest of the soldiers. 'Too old for war,' he once told me, and being so far from home had made him a little crazy. He couldn't get along with the young soldier they had given him to help him. He decided he wanted a local boy. Kline came to my father and my father recommended a boy of about fifteen. But he was the son of a *baalagolo* — a man who had a wagon and carried people from town to town, the minister of transport they would call him now — and the kid wasn't awfully bright and he got on Feldblum's nerves. After about two weeks Lieutenant Kline was back again, asking my father to recommend someone else. There wasn't much choice. All the boys of sixteen and over, including my older brother Jacob, had been taken by the Germans to help build the trenches. My father was mulling over a few possibilities when I walked in from school. Kline pointed to me and said, 'How about him?' My father said, 'He's only thirteen.' Kline answered, 'But he's sturdy and I know he's bright, just look at all the books he is carrying.'

"So the next day I began to work in the German bookstore. I had to sweep the floor and keep the wood stove going and tidy up Feldblum's spot in the back and sell newspapers and distribute the books. The men usually borrowed the books at first and sometimes, if they liked a book very much, they would buy it. I earned four marks, fifty pfennigs a week, and I learned how to read and speak German and how to run a bookstore. Feldblum liked me because I was willing and picked things up quickly. Knowing Yiddish helped; in very little time I was speaking and reading German.

"Feldblum had a second-class classification, because of his age I guess, but after three months he was called back to Germany and they sent Richard Hoffmann to take his place. Hoffmann had been given a third-class classification because he was partially deaf. He wore hearing aids in both ears. He was in his mid-thirties and very handsome and straight and tall — you can see that here in the picture." Herschel looked down at the photographs. "He was a brilliant man. He had been a librarian in Germany and this was his first field assignment. I helped him, and soon we had the bookstore running better than ever. We stayed in Olshan about eight more months.

"I used to get to the bookstore about eight in the morning and I stayed until almost six. On Friday afternoons I left early because it was the Sabbath and Papa was a rabbi and we were very observant. I never worked on Saturday, but I did have to go in on Sunday. And Hoffmann sometimes came to the house to visit and talk with my father. My mother liked Hoffmann and my sister Sarah, who was all of eleven at the time, used to wear her best clothes when he came. 'Hoffmann is very intelligent,' my father told my mother, and he didn't say that about many people.

"One day we heard that the border was to be moved

about twenty kilometers from Olshan. I had to go. I had never been away from home and my father was most worried about one thing: that I keep all the laws of Judaism. He told Hoffmann I was to do no work on the Sabbath and I had to put on my phylacteries — what we called 'lay t'fillin' — every morning and evening. Hoffmann gave my father his word.

"When the orders came the bookstore was scheduled to move on a Saturday morning. By then it was the beginning of winter, the end of nineteen sixteen, and this was very cold country. They were not going to send a wagon out the next day for one Jewish boy. But I couldn't ride because it was the Sabbath. So I walked beside the cart that carried Hoffmann, and as I walked Richard Hoffmann held my hand. For the entire eighteen kilometers. I will never forget that. Each time, after we had stopped for food or a drink, he would take my hand again and hold it in his.

"When we got to the village they put us and the books in this house." Herschel pointed to the second photograph. "You can see how rough it was on the outside; the boards weren't finished and it doesn't look like much, but it was tightly built, the cracks had been packed carefully with mortar. We were comfortable. We built homemade shelves and soon we had the store set up and running well. Then Hoffmann was told that I would have to go back to a farmhouse about five kilometers away every night to sleep because no civilians were allowed to sleep in the military facility. Hoffmann protested. It was bitter cold and I would have to make my way on an icy trail in the woods. But his protests were ignored. So I walked back and forth to the farmhouse for a few days. One morning Hoffmann didn't say anything, but simply set up a cot in the room next to his and told me to bring my clothes with me the next day. From then on I lived in the bookstore with him. Once the *Rittmeister* showed up early in the morning and I had my phylacteries on and was reciting the morning prayers. The *Rittmeister* pointed to the cot and raised his eyebrows. Hoffmann assured him that that was where I rested during the day. Then the *Rittmeister* came over to me and patted my head. *'Guten jugend,'* he told Hoffmann. *'Ja, Hersch es guten jugend,'* Hoffmann replied.

"Every night Hoffmann taught me what he knew. The first book we read together was by Jacob Wassermann, the German novelist, then we did Schiller and Goethe and Shakespeare and Aristotle and Homer and Plato. We spend weeks on the Allegory of the Cave; Hoffmann knew Greek and he loved the Greeks. He used to chant *The Iliad* to me. Did you know that Homer was meant to be sung?

"He also taught me algebra and geometry and biology and we read Newton and Saint Augustine's *City of God,* and I learned Montaigne and Pascal. He knew physics well, chemistry not so well, and we read Locke and Descartes and Spinoza, Hegel, even a little Kant. He also knew a lot about Jefferson. Years later, years and years after I came to America, I remember being utterly amazed when I saw the Jefferson Memorial and read the words 'I fear for my country when I reflect that God is just.' It was one of Hoffmann's favorite quotations.

"I stayed with Richard Hoffmann for a little more than three years and he taught me as much as he could. I went home to Olshan every few weeks for the weekend. They usually sent me in a wagon that was on its way to Vilna to get supplies. Before I left, Hoffmann would go around to the commissary and the post exchange and ask, 'Anything for the *jugend?*' They would give me old newspapers and all the denim I wanted.

"Yes, denim. The young people today think they've discovered it, but that's what the Germans used for the sandbags in the trenches. Their denim was good cloth, too, a lot sturdier stuff than they make jeans out of today, and everyone in Olshan soon had a skirt or a pair of pants made of denim.

"When I went home everyone was glad to see me. I had the papers and the denim, and as the war dragged on the Germans gave me large glass bottles of kerosene. That was against the rules, but the Germans were generous and didn't care much for rules, then.

"One day the *Rittmeister*, the same one who had patted me on the head that morning when I was saying my prayers, that *Rittmeister*—somehow I can't remember his name — came to Hoffmann. He wanted me to bring him a Polish woman who had followed the army and was now staying in Olshan. The woman was to walk back with me because it was too dangerous to send a carriage for her. A few rules were still strictly kept. Hoffmann gave me the woman's address. When I got home I showed my mother the slip of paper. She frowned but said nothing. When it was time for me to go back to the bookstore she wouldn't let me go to the address. She got up early that morning and got the woman. Then the woman and I walked back to camp." Now the thought of his mother, a rabbi's wife and well known in town, going into the red light district amused Herschel.

He smiled and began, "It was late summer . . ." Then

he fell silent. Suddenly the beautiful redhead was before his eyes. Surrounded by the hazy heat of that Russian summer she had been like a dream, even then. Strands of shimmering auburn hair kept escaping from the strip of silk she had used to tie it back. Bees and gnats dove for the lushness of her hair and she kept slapping them away, laughing all the time. Under her filmy white dress Herschel could see the outline of her breasts and her thighs. He began to have trouble swallowing. Once she brushed against him, and he got dizzy and thought he was going to be sick. But the nausea passed and he only began to understand it years later. Then he would fantasize about that day — what might have happened as he and the woman lingered in the high grasses, she laughing with a blade of grass between her teeth. Or later, in the cool shadowy forest when she had insisted they take their shoes off and dip their feet in a stream.

Now Herschel merely said to Laura, "She was very pretty and I was so dumb I had no idea why she was coming back to camp with me. She stayed a few days with the *Rittmeister*, then someone else walked her back to Olshan. After that the *Rittmeister* sent all sorts of things for me to take home — ersatz honey and ersatz butter and as much kerosene as we wanted. Although he never knew it, the *Rittmeister* kept the eternal light in our synagogue burning for almost three years.

"We were very isolated in that camp near the Beresina. When the German army pushed southward into the Ukraine and finally into the Crimea, they made our camp a depot. The Russian Revolution was beginning but we heard about it only through the German and Polish newspapers. After the Brest-Litovsk treaty we were virtually cut off from Russia. Food became scarce. During the last year of the war my family depended more and more on food I brought home with me from the camp. I would hide the food and kerosene in among the papers, or, occasionally, in the big hay wagons — among the bales of hay. Hoffmann knew what I was doing and he and some of the others helped me. Hoffmann was worried about my family and the Boyarskys and the rest of Olshan. He was afraid the people would starve. Years afterward, my mother said that they would have starved if it hadn't been for the German officers.

"All the time Richard Hoffmann and I lived together new books kept arriving from Germany, and Hoffmann continued to teach me. Every night after supper we sat down and read, then he would write questions and I would write answers to them. Then we discussed my answers — sometimes for hours.

"My father used to ask me what I was doing. Proudly I told him about the books and the discussions, but he only worried more. He thought all this knowledge would take me away from Judaism. I assured him that Hoffmann never let me do anything after sundown on Friday until sundown on Saturday. And I recited my prayers every single day.

"One Friday night in February of nineteen eighteen Hoffmann tried to make a fire in the wood stove. The wood had been laying outside, covered with snow. We used to pile it up in a shack near the cabin and the snow melted a little, but the logs were still sometimes crusted with ice and very wet. The trick is lots of kindling wood stacked in a series of triangles so that the air can get through. Then the wood will burn steadily. On this Friday Hoffmann must have been cold and in a hurry, because the cabin was filled with smoke. We were trying to eat and the smoke filled our nostrils and our eyes, even our ears. Hoffmann went out to get more kindling, but I could see that he hadn't piled it the right way. I took a poker and began to push the heavier logs off so that he could put the kindling on properly. When he came back and saw me poking that fire just after the Sabbath had begun, Richard Hoffmann got as pale as if he were watching a ghost. 'Hersch, Hersch,' he cried, 'what am I going to tell your father?'

"A promise is a promise, after all, and Hoffmann was an honorable man, one of the best men I ever knew. He had no children and after the armistice and all through the spring of nineteen nineteen while the army was packing up to go home he urged me to return to Germany with him. He and his wife wanted to adopt me. I had been his ears for almost four years. Before he left that summer he gave me both of these photographs and he wrote a message on the back of one." Herschel put on his glasses. Slowly he read the faded brown ink: " '*Zur Erinnerung an unser zusammen Arbeiten und an unser Kriegsquartier der Feldbuchhandlung Urljaty. Mit Liebe gewahren,* Richard Hoffmann.' " Then he translated it: " 'In memory of our working together and to our war quarters in the field bookstore in Urljaty. With love extended,' and there is something else, I can't quite make it out," Herschel said as he put the photograph down on the table.

"I was his ears for almost four years," he repeated "and, you know, his wife kept sending me all sorts of presents —

scarves and more books and sweaters and warm socks. Why once she even sent me a toothbrush."

On that detail the story ended. Herschel paused and looked out the window. His eyes were tired. Laura could see that he was still back in that dorf of almost sixty years ago. The effort of remembering events so far in the past had been a strain for him. As he dug deeper and deeper into his memory his speech had become more and more accented. By the end of the story all the *v*'s had become *w*'s and he had trouble finding the English for several words.

Herschel fingered the photographs and shook his head. He was glad Laura wasn't asking a lot of questions. He liked her for her ability to be quiet. A gift in a woman.

In telling the story he had remembered — with a sharpness that resembled pain — what he had thought his life would be like. Hoffmann and all that knowledge had made him feel he could conquer the world. Learning was more powerful than Arabian horses. But he was no different from hundreds of immigrants from Eastern Europe who had made some money and educated their children. And worse, he had not even communicated the past. A scrap here, a scrap there, but what did it all add up to? Nothing coherent, surely — a jigsaw puzzle with pieces missing. Could his children understand how he had felt when he opened a book he had never heard of before at a slab of a table in front of a crackling fire with Richard Hoffmann beside him? It seemed too much to ask — of himself and them. Yet he felt better for having told part of it. He looked at Laura.

Slowly she fingered the photographs. She had often wondered why her father had never told them about the concentration camps during World War II. She had been embarrassed by her innocence in the forties and had wanted to ask him why he, who was usually so open — especially about politics — had been so reticent about that. But she never had. And when she was in high school it was her mother who had told her that her Uncle Jacob, her father's older brother, had been killed with his wife and children at the beginning of the war. She looked up and met her father's eyes.

"I didn't want to believe any of it," he told her quietly. "Hitler was a lunatic, a sick man. I heard him speak in Munich in nineteen thirty-two — when I went back for a visit — and you could see it then. But he was only one man. That he accomplished his ends was incomprehensible to me. It still is. But Hitler wasn't the whole story, Laura." Now Herschel was his businesslike self again. He took the photographs and put them back into his billfold. Then he said firmly, "Anyway, it does no good to be obsessed about the past, we have the future to take care of."

The
Grandparents

THEY WALKED HUDDLED TOGETHER, HE SLIGHTLY
ahead of her, and the outline of those two little people in
black coats looked like one hunchback waiting to meet
God. Their son Herschel had wanted to help them into
the jet, but they refused. Slowly they walked up the boarding stairs, their eyes wincing in the bitter cold, onto the
plane that was to take them to Israel. He was eighty-five,
she eighty-six. They were moving because she had asthma
and found it hard to breathe in Brooklyn. His books had
been carefully packed and shipped to their new apartment
in B'nai Brock. Their clothes and personal effects filled
less baggage than most people take for a week's vacation.

I

For most of her life the grandmother, Henya Malka, had
been a working woman. She hated housework and did it
quickly and badly. She never learned how to cook a good
meal. A doctor once suggested that her bad cooking had

guaranteed the grandparents' longevity. They never seemed to look forward to a meal, and when one was put before them they ate indifferently. Henya Malka was far more interested in the newspapers and her husband's books than in recipes or the endless stories of confinement and childbirth other women seem to love. She had had eight uneventful pregnancies (she worked until the last week each time) and had delivered eight healthy children. She loved her children and cared for them, but she loved her store, too.

Like her illiterate mother, whom the people of Olshan had called "a walking abacus," Henya Malka was a merchant. More fortunate than her mother, she had gone to school and learned all kinds of useful things. Soon she became known for her ability to do impossible sums in her head. She also knew how to read Russian, Hebrew, Yiddish, and a little German. As the women entered her store they would hand their letters to Henya Malka. After they had picked out their groceries, or fingered the yard goods, or matched thread, they would come to the front, pay for their purchases, and listen to what their relatives and friends far away had written. Occasionally, a letter from France would arrive in the town and the recipient would rush to Henya Malka's store. She would try, but it was too hard. "The whole feel of the language is so different," she would explain to a crestfallen face. She even sent away for a French dictionary. But her next child was colicky and the days were too full.

While her children were babies and toddlers they spent most of the day in the playroom Henya Malka had made at the back of the shop. Books and toys tumbled from the shelves, and they had each other. When things were slow she read or sang to them. As they got older and went to *cheder* they stopped at the store on their way home. The boys helped her out during the busy afternoon hours, the girls went home to start dinner.

On market days, those busy noisy tiring days, Henya Malka and the children were happiest. Then the store became a small café. Tables were set up and draped with starched colorful cloths. Henya Malka had to fly! Thirsty, impatient tradesmen greeted her merrily as they gulped their beer. How exciting the talk was! Who wrote better, Chekhov or Tolstoi? Would there be a war after the suppression of the Boxer Rebellion? Who had advised Nicholas on Bloody Sunday? Did they know that Makhno was rumored to be hiding fifty miles away? Each market day, year after year, it was different, wonderful.

And later, far into the night, when the other women who couldn't sleep were doing needlework to soothe their nerves, Henya Malka went over her accounts — neatly, efficiently — not because she liked the money (she never had much feeling for money and preferred the kind of shopping that required very small amounts), but because she liked having the store and the stimulation it gave her. Besides, it would have done her no good if she had liked the money. As soon as she had totaled up the week's receipts on Thursday night, there was her husband, Avram Moshe, the rabbi, to collect them. He would clear the table and separate her allowance into small piles — so much for food, for rent, for the children's clothes, for incidentals.

Henya Malka didn't complain. She could never have stayed home and simply taken care of the house and children. After she came to this country in 1936 she always seemed a little wistful. Or lonely. She was sixty. Her three daughters and one son had gone to Palestine. She had come to America with her two youngest — boys of twenty and seventeen — and had joined her husband and second son. They were lucky to have gotten out of Olshan. She worried about her eldest, a rabbi like his father, who had chosen to stay near Vilna with his wife and babies. But her concern for the children far away wasn't the whole story. Henya Malka missed her store.

The store in Olshan was the constant in Henya Malka's life — children come and go and eventually leave. Sometimes, so do husbands. For Henya Malka's husband was a missionary rabbi who was often gone for many weeks at a time. Once he was away for three months. He wrote to tell her he would be home for a week, but then, unfortunately, he would have to leave again, he didn't know for how long. Henya Malka tried to think of a way to tell him he was planning to come home at the wrong time of the month. With some red ink she had found on a cluttered shelf in the storeroom she referred to the dates of his planned arrival home. He delayed his trip and appeared a week later.

Whether his comings and goings over the years had prepared Henya Malka for the day in 1927 when Avram Moshe walked slowly into the store, beckoned her to come into the back with him, and announced quietly that the next month he was leaving for America, no one ever knew. In 1905 her own father had returned to Russia after spending ten miserable months in New York. Not everyone loved America. Still, even ten months was a long time. It would be lonely without him. She was fifty-two years old, they had been married almost thirty years, she was finished having children. They both looked and felt younger than they were. The townspeople said she grew prettier each year. None of that helped. He had given her no warning. She stood there, stunned, as he outlined his plans. She kept listening for some sign of hesitation on his part. There was none. He had thought about this for a long time, and he had made up his mind to go.

II

Not even a blizzard could deter Avram Moshe. He had only so many days to get to Boulogne, where he would catch the boat that left for America. Through relentless, record-breaking winds and snow he journeyed from Olshan to Vilna and onto a train — first to Berlin, then to Boulogne — and finally aboard a large and crowded ship across the Atlantic Ocean until he reached Ellis Island. Most men would have been tired of traveling by then. Not he. He spent a few weeks with his son Herschel, who had come to America in 1920. Then, with the help of the official organization of Orthodox Jews in America, he began the trek across thousands of miles — a missionary rabbi with a thick graying beard, piercing blue eyes, in a longish black coat and hat. But not a fanatic. His beard was trimmed, he wore no *pais;* he smoked cigarettes, which he rolled himself and cut and stuck (a half at a time) into an engraved silver holder.

From New York to Knoxville to St. Louis to Denver and

even as far north as Vancouver he went, with a change of clothes, a few tall books that read from right to left, and his *t'fillin* which he caressed each dawn. He managed to find people who knew some Yiddish or Russian or German to give him food and company and a bed. Some who met him thought it a strange life for a man in his early fifties who had a wife and children so far away. Others thought it was a terrible thing for him to do. A few were more tolerant. Maybe he needed a place to think. Perhaps as he walked he dreamed of being Hillel or Moses Maimonides.

When asked about those early days in America, Avram Moshe said, "I lived." Then he would add, "Go to Lake Superior — beautiful."

In 1932 he settled down in Borough Park, Brooklyn, where he was given a synagogue of his own. Every few days Herschel would visit him. As soon as Avram Moshe heard his son's step in the hall he would slide the cover off the rectangular wooden box that held the chessmen. They had used that box since Hersch was a boy; now the sides of the cover felt like silk. After their chess game they talked — endlessly: of stylistic variations in the Book of Isaiah, the League of Nations, Spinoza, Herzl, the Talmudic interpretations of the Book of Job, Maimonides, Akiba, then Woodrow Wilson and Hitler.

Occasionally Hersch mentioned his mother, but his father seemed content and, strangely, so did Henya Malka in her letters to them both. A good son, Hersch didn't meddle. After Hersch married it was his wife, Frieda, who chided Avram Moshe.

"It's not right, you still have years and years together, a rabbi needs his wife, his *rebetzen*," she said.

History was on Frieda's side. It was becoming all too

clear that there was no future for Jews in Olshan. In 1935 Frieda and Hersch set about the complicated task of getting Henya Malka and Hersch's brothers and sisters out of Russia.

Three sisters and one brother went to Palestine. The two youngest boys came to Brooklyn with Henya Malka. Jacob, the eldest and a rabbi, refused to move.

Henya Malka arrived on a shimmering day in June. The photographs had the look of early Renoir paintings. Out of the confusion on the sunny pier suddenly materialized two boys of seventeen and twenty — bewildered, awed, uncomfortable already in their badly fitting clothes and prisonlike haircuts. Then Henya Malka, with the sun behind her, smiling proudly in her European black, her skirt too long and bunchy, her wrinkled kerchief in her hand as she waved to catch an eye. Then Herschel and Frieda, their hair so brown, Frieda's dress a flowered print with a gored skirt that swirled around her calves, Herschel in a dapper light suit and dark tie — all the worry of the past months gone from their eyes. And finally, Frieda and Henya Malka stepping tentatively toward each other.

Herschel and Henya Malka had the same brown eyes. "They called me 'Shining Eyes' when I was a girl," she once told Frieda.

III

Now, after almost ten years, Henya Malka had a husband again. On her way to America, as she had stood on deck and watched the endless ocean, she had wondered if they would try to fill in to each other all that had happened. Could they? Or would they just go on, never attempting to close the gap, knowing it was futile? In her mind she could hear them talking, but after her arrival very little was said about those years they had been apart. They looked the same to each other. To their relatives who observed them carefully those first few months they were together, they seemed content. He spent a lot of time in *shul,* praying and talking to his colleagues and students. She kept house and looked after her boys. But housework in Brooklyn was no better than housework in Olshan. Although she scooted through the rooms like a mechanical toy, a duster often in her hand, Henya Malka could never make their apartment look like much. The only plants that sat on the metal radiator covers were forlorn-looking, spiky things that pricked to the touch. What fascinated Henya Malka was the English language. While her sons went to learn it with the other Hyman Kaplans, she taught herself, so that within two years she was reading the *New York Times* as well as the *Jewish Daily Forward.*

For the first time in her life Henya Malka was a *rebetzen.* Her husband had a congregation. A white sign with his name in Hebrew letters appeared near the door of their four-family house. Their hallway was filled with the weary, the questioning, the troubled. In the years away from him she had forgotten Avram's seemingly infinite capacity for talk. Unnoticed, she would slip out with her string bag on her arm and go to Ninth Avenue. There, swept along by the noise, the smells, the variety of people, she shopped and chatted happily with each merchant — Yiddish or English as he preferred.

With her little topknot and quick smile Henya Malka looked like the perfect grandma, and now that she knew English she could be the perfect grandma to her American granddaughters. But that was a pleasure she denied herself and her grandchildren. For she and Avram Moshe refused to speak English to Hersch's daughters. They wanted Hersch and Frieda to teach the little girls Yiddish.

"Nothing doing," said Frieda, who had heard enough Yiddish to last a lifetime. As the last child of a large immigrant family and the only one who had had the good luck to be born in America, Frieda knew what she wanted for her girls. It certainly wasn't Yiddish. "Nothing doing," she said when they repeated their request. "This is America. English is spoken here."

The grandparents' insistence on Yiddish and Frieda's refusal to teach it to her children was a matter of principle. But it confused the grandchildren. Communication between the grandparents and grandchildren was a pantomime of guesswork, which made it impossible for the grandchildren to feel rooted in their grandparents' love. It also exasperated Hersch, who was continually in the middle, harassed by both sides, as he tried to translate and answer simultaneously.

Although he didn't talk to his granddaughters, Avram Moshe taught them the names of the chessmen in both Yiddish and English. After they learned the elementary moves, he waited patiently as they pushed out the pawns, then smiled when they gave up because the board had become too complicated and Hersch came to rescue them. Avram Moshe was also fond of "Round and Round the Garden" in Russian. As soon as the little girls had kissed him and been brushed by his beard in return, they would give him their palms. He would twirl his finger round and round, whispering the words, then tickle their forearms. He didn't play anything else with them. It was the only childhood game he knew.

One day early in 1940 Henya Malka and Avram Moshe rushed into Hersch's home; their faces were very pale, their hands trembled. It was already dark. He was usually at *miras* service in *shul,* she should have been safe in her kitchen preparing dinner. They thrust a telegram into Frieda's hand. She pressed her lips together as she dialed the phone to call Hersch. Soon he and his brothers were there. Before the night was out a crowd of people had gathered in the living room.

The next day and for the following week Henya Malka and Avram Moshe sat in their apartment on orange crates. They looked listless; occasionally a few words would dribble from their mouths. When someone persuaded them to eat they would take a bite from a cold bagel. Their son Jacob had died. As rabbi of a small village near Vilna he had called a meeting of the people and openly defied the Nazis. As an example to anyone else who might be so foolish, he and his wife and two children were shot in the village square.

After that week of *shiva* Henya Malka and Avram Moshe concealed their grief and adjusted to the reality of war. Their younger sons wanted to enlist. The youngest, always frail, was rejected by the draft board. The elder one was sent to North Africa, where he remained until the end of the war.

In the fall of 1942 Hersch and Frieda looked forward to the birth of their third child. Henya Malka and Avram Moshe were convinced it would be a boy. Frieda had little patience with them — a war was on and, besides, she was looking at houses in the suburbs. In September Hersch and his family moved from Brooklyn to Long Island. "How could you do this?" Henya Malka said. Avram Moshe stared coldly at his son. Avram Moshe saw this as one more indication of Frieda's misdirected zeal to make her children Yankees. Though his grandchildren were girls, Avram Moshe had become interested in their Hebrew educations.

"Where's the Orthodox *shul?*" he kept asking Frieda, but no one answered.

For Henya Malka it was simpler: Frieda was depriving her of her son. Since Jacob's death Henya Malka had become more protective; she worried about Hersch's health and safety. The knowledge that he was to live more than an hour away by train or car was more than she could bear.

Frieda and Hersch went to the hospital in a gray November dawn. When the little girls — Laura and Barbara — came home from school they could see their father's shadow in the living room. They had a new baby sister, named Erica. As they changed their clothes they could hear their father on the telephone; first his voice was quiet, then there were hoarse angry shouts. Laura went to the doorway of her parent's bedroom as he put down the phone. His face looked almost ugly. Then her father slumped down on the love seat and put his head in his hands and cried. The sight of his unhappiness frightened her beyond words. She ran for her life and never told a soul what she had seen.

Despite all her efforts to forget it, that scene came to visit Laura time and again. Eighteen years afterward, when Laura was expecting her first child, she visited Henya Malka and Avram Moshe. Henya Malka looked at Laura's swollen body carefully and said nothing. Avram Moshe was more forthright.

"If it is a boy," he said in English — for since Laura had married someone who didn't know Yiddish they finally talked to her in English — "please call me."

"And if it is a girl?" Laura asked.

"Don't bother," he muttered in Yiddish.

IV

After he moved to Long Island Hersch visited his parents almost every week. Sometimes the whole family came — Frieda and the three girls and Hersch — and sometimes Hersch brought Laura or Barbara or both older girls with him. They arrived around three. The long staircase up to the grandparents' apartment was dark and badly ventilated. A generation of cooking odors had seeped into its wood. The banister where Henya Malka stopped to catch her breath while carrying her groceries was worn smooth. The children ran up the stairs and she would wait for them at the top, peering down to make sure they had not lost their footing. Behind her the door to the apartment was ajar — it was always ajar except when she and Avram

Moshe closed it each summer to make the pilgrimage to Rockaway. As each of them reached the top step Henya Malka would hold their faces briefly in her hands, then she would scurry into the kitchen, hoist herself onto a wobbly white chair, and grope in the highest glass-doored cabinet for the candy. For the adults there was fruit; if it was bitter cold, coffee and cake. For the children there was candy and raisins and nuts.

As they took off their hats and coats Avram Moshe would emerge from his study, holding a book in his hand. He would point to a phrase and tell Hersch what he thought about it and then return the book to his desk. The children rarely went into the study. It was forbiddingly spare: a high-backed wooden chair and a large slab desk and a few folding chairs propped against the closet door for visitors. Cabinets holding hundreds of books lined the walls; behind the glass doors were endless faded gold Hebrew letters on thin green or black or maroon spines.

Everyone sat in the living room. Hersch and his father soon disappeared into their weekly game of chess. The children alternately watched the game and listened to Frieda and Henya Malka. Thus the granddaughters learned early that women talk to other women, even if they disagree on the most fundamental rules for running a house. Frieda never got used to the drabness of Henya Malka's apartment or the slipshod quality of her housekeeping. Yet she found her mother-in-law interesting. Besides, though neither would admit it and often cluttered their lives with petty complaints against the other, the unspoken love they felt for each other was central to them both. When they were still small, the children recognized that love, just as they recognized the love between Hersch and his parents, and that's why they never minded the Sunday afternoon visits, even if they were sometimes too hot, or chilled, or tired, or hungry, or too full.

While the two women talked Henya Malka never sat back in a chair or sofa; she simply rested on its edge, ready to move if someone needed something or if she wanted to show Frieda a news article she had clipped or a passage in something she was reading. After they had talked for a while Henya Malka would begin to smooth the girls' hair and straighten their clothes. That meant it was time to go next door, then downstairs, to visit the neighbors.

"How pretty they are! How they've grown! Their clothes are so lovely!" Each time it was the same, Henya Malka smiling and nodding, the children trying not to feel sick from the sweets that were being pressed on them.

At about five they left. If the whole family had come they then visited Frieda's sister, who lived three blocks away. There they were welcomed into an immaculate white kitchen where the table was set with a freshly laundered cloth, and they sat down to a wholesome, nourishing meal. Frieda was always angry that she had to come to her sister's for supper; she felt Henya Malka could make dinner for them now and then. But Henya Malka had cooked a big midday meal, and with candy and fruit all you needed was a snack before bedtime. The only food Henya Malka ever gave Frieda was an occasional jar of chicken fat, sometimes still warm from being cradled in her lap on the train ride to Long Island.

When the weather was mild, Henya Malka and Avram Moshe would make the trip to Long Island. First they took a subway, then a train, then Hersch would meet them at the station with the car. Occasionally they took an early train and walked the three long blocks from the station. Once Laura was practicing the piano when they arrived without any warning. When she looked up, they were standing quietly in the entrance to the living room. She had no idea how long they had been there. In their eyes were admiration and respect. Laura always played for them when they came, but this was different; they had caught her working and that gave them enormous pleasure.

In his own way Avram Moshe was working all the time. It looked like talking, but in the end it was his work. Every few years Hersch would announce that Grandpa had published another article in an erudite Orthodox journal — in Hebrew. Although his granddaughters could recite the Hebrew words easily, they had no notion what they meant. Avram Moshe was right. Their Hebrew education — if that's what you chose to call it — was all show.

Summers Avram Moshe and Henya Malka left Brooklyn and went to Rockaway. There, in a room and a half, and each year in a different house — all ramshackly and sparsely furnished (sometimes with no more than a table, a few wooden chairs and a bed) — they sacrificed the small comforts of their apartment for the cool ocean breezes. Frieda was always unhappy when she saw their summer places.

"They can afford better, they don't have to look as if they're camping out," she would say to Hersch, but Henya Malka and Avram Moshe didn't mind. They loved the sea; just sitting on the porch on hot summer nights and smelling the salt air made the rest worthwhile. Besides, they knew lots of people there; as they strolled on the boardwalk they were greeted with smiles and hellos.

One muggy afternoon Laura went with Hersch to visit them. Henya Malka was waiting in front of the house.

"Pa's not feeling well," she told Hersch. "He went for a walk and was supposed to be back for tea an hour ago." She frowned. "You go look. I'll wait here," she instructed.

Hersch and Laura walked quickly through a maze of black coats. At the boardwalk they went in opposite directions, planning to meet at the starting place in fifteen minutes. Laura walked along slowly, looking for a white beard and a pair of unexpectedly bright blue eyes. Just as she was about to turn around and go back to meet Hersch she saw a figure sitting on a bench. Something about the way he held his head made her stop. He got up and went to the boardwalk railing. His walk was a shuffle. Then he sat down on a bench near the railing. By now she was looking directly at him but he didn't notice her. His eyes looked so empty — more the color of slate than blue. He stared at the sea for several minutes. Gently Laura touched his arm; his eyes brightened. Then they walked slowly back for tea. Avram Moshe was very tired, almost sluggish.

"He must have a bug," Frieda said when they told her.

"No, he said he was having trouble with an article. He's just depressed," Hersch answered.

Then Avram Moshe was almost eighty. That he might be seriously ill seemed not to have occurred to either Hersch or Frieda. Laura couldn't understand how they could be so casual about it, but she didn't say anything that might worry them. Of course they were right. Within a few days Avram Moshe was feeling fine, and months later when the article was published he and Hersch laughed about the problems he had had with it.

After Laura was married her grandparents visited her once. Henya Malka touched every piece of furniture, every curtain, every ashtray. "The books should be in enclosed cabinets," she said. Laura shrugged and served them strong tea in heavy glass beer mugs. They praised her hospitality. They liked her husband and forgave him for being a Reformed Jew. "He is good as well as intelligent," Henya Malka told Hersch.

While Henya Malka and Avram Moshe lived in Israel, Laura and her husband and small daughter spent a year in London. Laura thought about going to see her grandparents, yet at the time Europe seemed so much more important; Israel could wait. But her grandparents were old and would have liked the visit. He was eighty-nine, she was ninety. He still spent his mornings writing; she straightened up the apartment and went to the marketplace every day. A lady came in to do the heavy work. The children in Israel visited them regularly, and sometimes for a treat Avram Moshe and Henya Malka would go to their daughter's café in one of the busiest sections of Tel Aviv for a glass of tea.

"It reminds me of the store," Henya Malka would say.

On Friday afternoons their son Schmul stopped on his way home from work with flowers for his mother. She sniffed and touched them all week. But the best times of the year were the visits from Hersch and Frieda. Then Henya Malka and Avram Moshe relaxed completely, as they never seemed to be able to do with these children in

Israel who had been through so much without them. Henya Malka's eyes grew almost black with contentment when they visited Elat, Haifa, Safed, Masada, and, best of all, Jerusalem.

It was a simple life, uneventful, but remarkable in its lack of illness or catastrophe. The grandchildren had children; on Rosh Hashanah and Pesach pictures of the babies and toddlers arrived. Henya Malka's purse bulged with them, for she couldn't bear to throw any away. Yet, toward the end, it was a life too long.

"I know it is ungrateful," she wrote to Hersch in her steady Hebrew hand, "but it is enough. I feel like the last leaf on the oak tree in winter. God has forgotten me." She was ninety-four, she walked very slowly, her breathing was labored, she was weary.

The following June she entered their apartment and put down her groceries for the day on the hall table. "Avram, please get me a glass of water," she said in a normal, clear voice. Then she leaned against the wall.

"Just a minute," he said. "I have to finish something."

She fell quietly to the floor.

"I killed Mama," he told his American sons when they arrived in B'nai Brock for the funeral. No one took him seriously.

Avram Moshe lived for another year and a half. His book was published by the best publisher of religious books in Tel Aviv. The longest article in it was an essay on divorce and Judaism. It gave him more recognition in Orthodox circles in both Israel and Brooklyn. At a funeral of a cousin someone mentioned to the officiating rabbi that Laura was Avram Moshe's eldest grandchild.

"Ah, he was a remarkable man. Very learned. Have you read his last book?"

"Yes," Laura lied, for this rabbi would not have understood how, in two generations, her life had become so different from her grandfather's.

The next time Laura visited her parents she asked to see Avram Moshe's book. Her father brought it to the dining room table. He also carried a photograph of Henya Malka and Avram Moshe and put it on the table next to the book. The book was bound in burgundy leather and on the slim side. Slowly, in Hebrew, Laura read the title, the author, the publisher. She turned the page.

"What's that?" she asked.

"The dedication," Hersch said. Then he read: "I dedicate this book to the memory of my wife of more than sixty years. Without her help and patience and devotion I could not have written it."

"It wasn't like him," Hersch said.

Frieda nodded. "And he always walked faster than she could. Look." She pointed to the photograph. The grandparents were walking down the aisle at Barbara's wedding. Henya Malka was dressed in her best clothes — a navy dress down to her ankles with a fine white lace collar and cuffs. A small hat perched on her white hair. Her eyes were opals, her chin was firm, a happy half-smile teased her lips. Avram Moshe was slightly ahead of her, very solemn, looking straight ahead. Marriage is a sacred ritual, his eyes-that-seemed-to-know-everything said. But hidden, almost out of the photograph, was his hand — reaching for, then grasping, hers.

V

Avram Moshe loved his books and, in his way, his wife and children, but he also loved money. That's why he loved America. Here a canny man could make a million. Here there was a stock market. As soon as he had gotten settled in Brooklyn in 1932, Avram Moshe found the druggist on Ninth Avenue whose nephew was a stock-broker. Every month or so a young man appeared at the door after dark, presented his bill, and was paid in cash.

Where did a rabbi get the money during the Depression to buy stocks? It was simple. Around the first of each month Hersch would linger as he left his father's apartment. In the dreary hall that smelled of tangerines, whatever the season, Avram Moshe handed his son the bills from the landlord and the gas, electric and telephone companies. With the money saved from that monthly transaction with his son, Avram Moshe bought IBM, Best & Company, American Tobacco, Georgia Pacific, AT&T. He had good advice. Most of the stocks climbed steadily upward, split, and climbed again.

Although he thought he was keeping his fancy investments a secret, Henya Malka knew exactly what he was doing and she knew it was wrong. When a dividend check came she threw it away. Then he would have to go down to the garbage pail at night and sift through the slops to retrieve it, he hoped not ruined. But Avram Moshe didn't care. After it had happened several times he stayed home and waited for the mail when he knew the checks would be coming.

For Henya Malka the money from the stocks was always tainted. What you worked for was fine; with that you could buy warmth or comfort or pleasure when you could afford it. Money that simply arrived in the mail was bad. That she couldn't understand the potentialities of the stock market was everlasting proof to Avram Moshe that she would never be as American as he was.

Her basic objection was not really to the stock market. It was to the idea of taking money from one's son for necessities and at the same time investing in stocks. But the morality of what he was doing never seemed to have occurred to Avram Moshe, or, if it did, he had found a way out of the dilemma that he never shared with his wife or anyone else. He was a modern man; golden calves belonged to the past.

Henya Malka and Frieda and, later, his granddaughters would not have minded his financial finagling so much if Avram Moshe had become generous. But generous was something he didn't know how to be. Hersch was never relieved of his monthly obligations. No gifts appeared when they might have — on birthdays and anniversaries or each year at the Seder.

In late March or early April the grandchildren rushed home from school without even noticing the drifts of daffodils and hyacinths under the trees, without longing to ride their bikes to the pond or the park or the still-empty stretches of land on Long Island's south shore. For those were the Seder days, and they had to bathe and dress and join the huge line of traffic on the Belt Parkway into Brooklyn. The Seder started the moment Venus appeared in the sky; they couldn't be late. No matter how pressed Frieda was, the children always wore new clothes to the Seder. As soon as they arrived their aunts and uncles and cousins would admire their new outfits. Henya Malka would hurry from the kitchen and kiss them and rub the cloth of their dresses between her small shapely fingers, then nod to Frieda in approval. The living room of the grandparents' apartment had been transformed. Around a huge oval table set with a white damask cloth were an extraordinary number of faces: a man and a woman both named Alta, Jennies, Lazars, Davids, a Max and a Sam, and Roses, Harrys, Hannahs, a Beatrice and a Mary. Wine glasses were reflected in eyeglasses. The refracted candlelight multiplied with each sip of wine. On that night Olshan seemed to have been transported to Brooklyn. Every word of the Passover *Haggadah* was intoned, often debated. It took over an hour to get to the Four Questions, which the children read faultlessly. It took hours more to get to the meal. But before that was the hiding of the *Afikomen,* the piece of matzoh that literally means dessert.

Avram Moshe sat on the traditional mound of pillows during the Seder. When Henya Malka came with a basin for him to wash his hands, he turned toward her and performed the ritual slowly, to give the children time. As soon as one of them had stolen the *Afikomen* and slipped it behind a chair or table, the fantasies would begin. For the Seder could not end without the *Afikomen,* and to get it back the leader of the Seder gave those who could produce it a prize. Thoroughly Americanized, the children would wonder: Should they ask for a doll or a game, or something as large as a radio, or, possibly, a new bicycle? With his blue eyes twinkling behind his bifocals and a contented smile on his face, their grandfather seemed capable of giving presents he had never given before.

"What would you like?" Avram Moshe would ask, and the children would articulate their wishes — at first shyly, then, as they were being encouraged, more confidently.

But each year it was the same. A few bills thrust into the children's hands by Hersch, who couldn't bear to watch the exchange any longer. Sometimes the children waited up past midnight to open the door for Elijah, sometimes they went to sleep — more from disappointment than from tiredness — and were awakened to a strange melancholy singing of *Had Gadya* they were never to hear again. It matched their mood as the women dressed them and the men of the family carried them out to the car in the early hours of the following morning. When they went back to school after the spring holiday the children would always brag that they had stayed out latest at their grandfather's Seder.

Occasionally Avram Moshe gave away money. But never without a lecture. At Laura's wedding supper the house was like a furnace at 11:30 at night. A wildcat subway strike had delayed the small wedding and the meal was hours behind schedule. As the dessert plates were being cleared, Avram Moshe rose with an envelope in his hand. He talked about the responsibilities of marriage, the sanctity of the relationship between men and women in the Jewish religion. Hersch stood behind Laura and her husband and translated. Two huge fans recirculated steamy air; everyone but Avram Moshe was exhausted. Finally he stopped and handed Laura an envelope. It was the awkward gesture of a man not used to giving.

And when Barbara gave birth to the first great-grandchild, it was, miraculously, a boy. There was a *pidyon ha ben*, a celebration for the first male in a family. More than fifty friends and relatives crowded into the living room of Frieda and Hersch's home. It was March, snow flurried outside, people were getting anxious about leaving, but Avram Moshe was oblivious. Again he held an envelope in his hand and lectured Barbara and her husband and everyone else on the deep and sacred obligations of parenthood in Judaism. It was 1959. Avram Moshe was almost eighty-three years old. He had just played a long game of chess with Hersch and had won. He looked sixty-five; his mind flew from thought to thought with incomparable ease. He was becoming a legend in his own time, so normal standards didn't apply.

By then Hersch's business was a success. As a reward for his hard work and forebearance he was now expected to pay not only Avram Moshe's rent and utilities, but for some of his investments as well. Every now and then a young man who spoke only Yiddish would appear at Hersch's office on lower Broadway with a bill for stocks bought under the family name. After much gesturing someone would go for Hersch, who then called his father on the telephone. Avram Moshe insisted impatiently that it was perfectly fine, Hersch should pay the bill, they would settle it later. Hersch always paid and hoped Frieda wouldn't find out. Of course, settlement day never came.

VI

In 1962 Avram Moshe's American dream came to an end. Henya Malka's asthma had made it impossible for her to spend another winter in Brooklyn; they were moving to Israel. They had bought a new apartment in B'nai Brock when they went for a visit to Israel; they had ordered new furniture and were now returning to the children they had not known for at least a generation. There were grandchildren to get to know, a whole new country to explore. Henya Malka was happier than she had ever been since she left Olshan. Avram Moshe was miserable. He didn't want to leave his *shul*, his cronies, the respect he had earned as a scholar and rabbi emeritus. The minute he walked out of the door of his house in Brooklyn people stopped, grateful for an opportunity to speak to him. A few of the more fanatic and lonely women in the neighborhood were in the habit of kissing his hand. It was all hard to leave. So were his investments. He liked watching them grow. But he had no choice.

The first thing he did in Israel was to vent his anger on the Israeli Customs Authority. He refused to pay forty dollars duty on their new refrigerator. It lay crated on the dock for three months until Henya Malka finally wrote to Hersch in anguish. Hersch used her letter as an excuse to visit them; of course he paid the duty.

Avram Moshe was disappointed in his children in Israel. They were not religious and they seemed too interested in material things. "All they want is my money," he wrote to Hersch and Frieda. One wanted a bigger refrigerator, another needed a new stove, the third daughter had had a nervous breakdown after the War for Independence in 1948 and needed psychiatric care. He was expected to pay. He recognized the need to help them, though constitutionally it was hard for him. Plagued by their needs, he parted with very little. On his yearly, then twice-yearly trips to Israel, Hersch tried to placate his sisters and brother.

"He's old," Hersch said.

"He's stingy," they retorted.

After Henya Malka died Avram Moshe tried to live alone, but then he developed cancer of the larynx and had to have his voicebox removed. He went to live with his second daughter. She insisted he pay for his room and food. He was appalled.

"All she cares about is my money," he wrote. Bewildered, he kept shaking his head. He was not a man to notice shabbiness or even poverty; he assumed everyone could live as simply as he did — with a chair and a table and books and a little food. He was depressed by the loss of his voice — that was a privation these children had no notion of. Besides, they would have their share of his estate when he was dead. But that was not enough for his Israeli children. They had lived through severe hardships, wars; now they, too, were getting older. Wasn't it time for a little comfort?

Their demands exceeded his patience. He saw no relationship between his children's actions and his own life. If he had looked up one day and seen that original handwriting on the wall, MENE, MENE, TEKEL, UPHARSIN, he would not, even then, have made the connection. He had looked in the mirror for almost a hundred years and had never found himself wanting. Slowly Avram Moshe became angrier and angrier. Finally he wrote to his lawyer and several weeks later, in a whisper, dictated a new will. He left everything he had to an interest-free money-lending agency in B'nai Brock. When his will was read his children in Israel refused to believe it. For years afterward they were still fighting it in a court in Tel Aviv.

At the same time that he dictated his new will Avram Moshe wrote to his oldest grandchild in America — Laura. When their third child was born, Laura and her husband had named the baby girl after Henya Malka, and although Avram Moshe was not in the habit of sending gifts at the births of great-grandchildren, this baby was special. He intended to get a check in the mail as soon as he heard about the baby's birth. But he didn't. Suddenly he heard that the baby was two years old. He could scarcely believe that two years had passed so quickly and he knew he risked making a fool of himself by sending a gift so late, but some unknown compulsion forced him to sit down and write a letter. His handwriting was stilted, as it always was when he wrote in English: "Dear Laura, Mama and Papa tell me your little girl is growing nicely. I hope you have enormous pleasure in raising her. And I hope she is as lovely as her name. Your grandfather, A.M." He attached a check to the letter.

Laura deposited the check in the bank and wrote her grandfather a thank-you note.

The following spring Herschel and Frieda went to Israel and saw Avram Moshe for the last time. He still got dressed every day and read and studied and whispered. His eyes were still amazingly bright; he had grown accustomed to being quite deaf early in his nineties, but his inability to speak was more than he could stand.

"All my life I have lived by talking," he explained to Hersch, who tried to comfort him. And then they would whisper slowly to each other, for Hersch found it hard to speak in a normal voice when his father was having such difficulty.

After Hersch got back to New York he called Laura. "Are you there?" he said; it was his substitute for "hello." Then, before she could even ask how he was, he said, "Grandpa says he never received a note from you acknowledging his letter and check."

"I wrote him within a week," Laura replied.

"Oh, well, perhaps his memory is going," Hersch said, and added softly, "He's ninety-six already." Hersch's voice was sad, and as Laura heard it she knew that Hersch was preparing himself for Avram Moshe's death. It came, quietly, two months later.

The next fall Laura pulled on her old jacket, the one she used for little else but garden work. Her children were helping her pile the leaves into large plastic bags. One of them sneezed. She dug into her pocket for a Kleenex and pulled out the letter to Avram Moshe — addressed and stamped to go to Israel. When Laura next saw Hersch she showed him the letter. His eyes glowed with a mixture of relief and delight. "He always had a good memory," he said.

An
Easy Life

GENYA AND LAZAR KAPLAN ARRIVED IN AMERICA THE
week that Einstein won the Nobel Prize. Their cousin
Herschel met them at the pier. All they could talk about
was Einstein; his triumph seemed a blessing on them. And
although they finally answered Herschel's questions about
the deaths of their parents and sister, it was clear that
death and Olshan were behind them. They were alive, and
in New York.

Lazar was twenty-three; he had been trained as a dentist
in Vilna. He would take the examinations and then set up
a practice. For Genya the cousins had chosen a lawyer's
son, but she had other ideas. She was determined to be a
doctor.

"But you're only eighteen, you're too young to know
what you want; Jewish girls don't become doctors, not
even in America. Besides, you can't even speak English,"
the relatives said to her in Yiddish.

"I'll learn," she replied.

Genya and Lazar settled a few blocks from Herschel's
family in Brooklyn. Soon Lazar had a thriving practice. He
was bright and likable and very ambitious. While Genya

kept house for her brother she learned English in record time. In September she enrolled in Brooklyn College, and soon the whole neighborhood knew she intended to go to medical school. She always had a book with her; as she waited her turn at the butcher's or the greengrocer's she would read. With her short red hair and deep green eyes she looked like no other Jewish girl in all of Brooklyn. You could spot her blocks away.

"There goes Genya. Someday she'll break a leg, reading and walking at the same time," said the old men who sat in front of the drugstore.

"She'll meet a man. Then she'll change her high and mighty ways," the women told their children. They were wrong. She met a man, she met a few men and probably fell in love more than once, but she was not just going to be someone's wife. In the spotless cozy house in Olshan she had watched her parents put each other to bed and finally die of influenza. Despite warnings of her own death she had held her sister while the Jews of Olshan prayed endlessly for three days and three nights. But the little girl died, too. Genya had lain, sick herself and so helpless with grief that she had almost died, but when she finally recovered she promised herself that she was never going to feel so helpless again.

Lazar married Hannah Kahn. The richest woman in the neighborhood. Ten years older than he was, but handsome, and they were fond of each other. They had a wedding with five bridesmaids and a flower girl and Hannah's father bought them a nine-room house with white pillars in Borough Park. For another two years Genya lived with them. Then she went to live with a distant cousin in Man-

hattan near NYU Medical School. They had accepted her
— a woman and a Jew. They had no choice. She was vale-
dictorian of her class at Brooklyn and she could pay her
way.

Genya's determination was now admired, praised. When
people who didn't know her met her they couldn't believe
that such a slight and unassuming girl was Genya Kaplan.
Success made her gentler; though she was still serious she
had more of a sense of humor than she had had a few years
ago. Medical school wasn't as hard as everyone had warned.
The summer after her first year she came home to Lazar's
with a flute. She was going to learn lullabies for her new
nephew. In the mornings the neighbors heard her practice.

"So now she wants to lead the symphony orchestra,"
they told Lazar when they came to get their teeth fixed.

"Leave her alone," he said indulgently. He loved Genya
more than anyone in the world — more than his wife, more
than his son. He would make the money, let her be happy.
He never worried, as Hannah did, about Genya marrying.

"When she wants a husband she'll have one." Meantime
he loved hearing her play her flute. When she became
better at it she joined a chamber music group. Once a
week she came home and the group played in Lazar's living room. To him this was the epitome of his success in
America. He bought a Steinway. After the music Hannah
served fancy meals from steaming silver chafing dishes.

Genya graduated from medical school in 1929. Lazar
gave her money to set up a clinic in lower Manhattan and
came down himself to watch the workmen repair the old
apartment she had rented. When they were almost finished
he showed them where to place the bronze plaque on the

outside of the building. He had had it made himself. It read, EUGENIE KAPLAN, M.D. Genya was unhappy. Although her diploma said Eugenie and that was her real name, she had wanted to be known as Genya. It seemed right for her. But she could hardly ask him to change it she thought, as she watched his face while the men nailed the plaque into the brick.

The stock market crashed. Hannah's family lost their money. Lazar had to sell his house and move to an apartment, though they were still well off by any standard. He kept the Steinway; his son had begun to play, and a few years later Hannah gave birth to a baby daughter who would play, too.

Genya's practice grew, but the money came in very slowly. Most patients could pay only a token fee; still, Genya was doing what she wanted. After two years she had accumulated enough money to rent a tiny apartment of her own near the clinic. Every other week she went home to Lazar's for dinner; in her handbag was a small check. She intended to pay him back for her schooling, and though he didn't want it he knew he couldn't dissuade her.

When Genya went home it was a celebration. The children adored her. First she would play her flute for them; then they would open her small thoughtful presents. After she had put them to bed the neighbors would flock in — some with complaints, some just to see her. For the sick she wrote prescriptions; to the well she listened. Some had a man for her. Others criticized her clothes.

"You're too small to wear capes," one woman told her.

"I like them," she replied. Lazar had to admit she

dressed a little oddly for a Jewish girl; she seemed to fancy all those loose dramatic things that were made for tall women, but he also had to admit that she could bring them off. Her small slim figure had grace, her red hair had browned a little but was still striking, and her eyes glowed, even when she was being criticized.

Finally she called Hannah and asked if she could bring a guest to dinner. His name was William Wollman and he was a lawyer. At first Lazar wasn't sure he was Jewish, but soon Genya had shifted the conversation to Colonial America and Bill told them his ancestors had been among the first Jews to settle in William Penn's colony. His home was in Philadelphia, but as soon as he graduated from Penn Law School he had come to New York. He loved the city as much as Genya did.

Genya had found her husband. When she looked at Bill she reminded Lazar of their mother. As a child he was sometimes embarrassed by the way his parents had looked at each other, and here it was again. Only this time he was not embarrassed, maybe a little envious. Genya seemed to have everything.

When they left he called a friend who was a caterer. "Start planning. I give them about six weeks." Exactly a month later Genya and Bill went to city hall. Lazar never got over his disappointment. He had daydreamed her wedding so many times that each gesture would have been perfection. He had to content himself with a large and exquisite reception, but he felt that Genya had denied him a great pleasure — to give her away in a Jewish ceremony under a *chupa*, a wedding canopy, of camellias.

In a few years Genya was invited to teach at NYU because her clinic was becoming a famous example of how a good general practice can work despite the trend toward specialization. Bill opened his own law firm. They had a large apartment on Central Park West. They still saw Lazar and Hannah and the children every few weeks, but Lazar missed the chamber music. Genya had found a group in Manhattan; she invited him to come and listen in her apartment. It wasn't the same.

Lazar worried that she wouldn't have children. Once when they had taken his children to the zoo he pointed to a monkey nursing her babies. "So . . . when is the lady doctor going to have little doctors?" She smiled and didn't answer, but Lazar knew from her expression that there were no problems.

The day after Roosevelt was elected for his second term Genya Kaplan had triplets. "She never could do anything like anyone else," her relatives said when they came to the *bris*, for two were boys. The little girl, whom they named Rachel after Genya's sister, was very frail. Each afternoon Genya could feel a catch in her throat as she walked to the apartment, wondering if she was still alive. When the babies were three months old Genya tried staying home all the time and letting an assistant run the clinic, but Rachel didn't pick up weight. When she was seven months old she got pneumonia and died.

Genya was miserable. She had thought she would never have that feeling again, but it was as if she were still a girl in Olshan. When Lazar got to the hospital she was holding the dead child in her arms, her face smeared with tears. She was mourning for her parents and her sister and her daughter. After the funeral Lazar was worried. Genya walked as though her body were a sack she had to carry around; she took to wearing grays and browns. Soon Lazar found himself taking no appointments after three in the afternoon. Then he would rush to the subway and go down to Genya's clinic. By four, when he arrived, she was finished for the day; she usually used the last hour for paperwork. When Lazar came she would smile, they would have tea, and they would talk — of their parents, Olshan, their friends from childhood, the ones who had stayed and the ones who had come to America. Those weeks were among the happiest of Lazar's life; after several months he breathed easier.

Gradually Genya was becoming famous. Her practice changed as the neighborhood around her changed, and after the war she became an authority on sickle-cell anemia, the disease of her black patients. Neighbors brought magazine articles and newspaper clippings about her to Lazar; these he pasted carefully into leather-bound scrapbooks. Whenever Genya went to lecture somewhere she sent him a postcard with a note about how the lecture had gone and what the city was like. Her boys played with his children on family holidays, and when Lazar's daughter said she wanted to study medicine Genya wrote her recommendations to several medical schools. She got into Yale the same week that her mother, Hannah, began to complain of stomach pains. Now it was Genya's turn to sit with Lazar. She met him at Mount Sinai every afternoon; together they watched Hannah die of intestinal cancer. As Lazar saw her coming toward him one hot afternoon he noticed, for the first time, how streaked with white her hair was. She was only fifty-three. Her upper arms were a little heavier than he remembered, but the rest of her was still very slight. Her face was covered with perspiration. She saw him looking at her.

"We're middle-aged, Lazar." She wiped her face with a Kleenex. "And I have been perspiring steadily for six months."

He patted her arm. "That, too, will pass."

After Hannah's death Genya asked Lazar to come live with her and Bill. His son was a lawyer and married; he and his wife lived in the Midwest; his daughter had an apartment in New Haven. Their boys were away at college. They had plenty of room in their old apartment on Central Park West and excellent help. "It would be wonderful to have you," Genya said. Of course Lazar refused. He had his practice in Brooklyn, his friends, his enormous record collection. "I'll manage," he said.

Lazar's daughter became a pediatrician and married an internist. Their first child was a girl whom they named Rachel. Lazar called Genya with the news, and a few days later she met him on the northeast corner of Sixtieth Street and Madison Avenue. He wanted her to help him pick out a gift for his newest granddaughter.

That day Genya was wearing a lovely navy cape. Her hair was almost white, but her eyes still had that stubborn look of her youth and their green still startled strangers. She and Bill were leaving for Europe in a few days. They had both been invited to lecture in England for several months and they had rented a small flat in Cambridge.

After she and Lazar kissed, Genya took his arm and they walked slowly, window-shopping a little at first. They finally found a woolly sack for the baby. "It will last all winter," Genya assured him. Then they went to a quiet restaurant for lunch. One would have thought she had all the time in the world. They talked of Lazar's practice, which was quite slow, whether he should retire completely, what he would do. They discussed their children — Lazar's son and daughter, and Genya's boys. One was a physicist doing work in Boston, the other was a doctor working in a clinic in London. Genya looked forward to seeing him when they arrived in England.

Lazar was happy for her. And, as usual he felt better after he had seen her. The day had gotten cloudy and windy. As they left the restaurant someone said, "It looks like snow."

The windy city looked bleak to Lazar. "New York's changing," he murmured. Genya looked at him in surprise.

"It was always dismal on days like this, Lazar. No, New York is the same; it's the most wonderful city in the world," she chided him. Her voice was so sure of itself he had to smile. Then Genya turned to him.

"You go now, the subway's right here. I don't want you to get caught in the snow. I'll catch a cab and hop down to the clinic for a while. Bill has to work late." She kissed him on both cheeks, then turned up his collar against the wind. When he got to the bottom of the subway stairs he turned. She was waiting. He waved and she blew him a kiss. She was smiling.

Within a few minutes after Genya got into the cab she knew that the cabbie had voted for Kennedy, that he had four kids, that he played the French horn in a small symphony orchestra in New Jersey.

"You also drive too fast," she scolded him.

"Yeah, I suppose so, but it keeps me awake. This job is pretty boring," he said.

When they stopped he turned around to look at her. "And what do you do?" he asked as she was paying him.

"Oh, me, I have lunch with my brother and take very good care of my husband now that the children are grown." But she wasn't fooling anyone.

" 'Bye, missus, and good luck," the cabbie called as she got out and slammed the door. They were right in front of the plaque with her name. Age had streaked it green.

Whistling loudly as he took off, the cabbie gunned the car as usual. Passersby screamed. By the time he was able to stop he had dragged Genya a few hundred feet. She was unconscious and a shred of her cape was still in the door. When she woke up she was in her hospital, one side shattered.

Genya tried to be gay when people came to visit but she could barely speak. If she made the effort to say a few words the pain became unendurable. Lazar couldn't believe it. He had never seen her in bed since they came to America. Now, to see her like this. So tiny and broken, she was a gnome.

He came every day. He read aloud to her in Russian: Chekhov, Turgenev, Akhmatova, Pasternak. He pointed out the inconsistencies in time in *Dr. Zhivago*. "At times it reads like a dream," he explained. Genya smiled to show him she could still care. For a while the doctors predicted a wheelchair. Then, at the end of the summer, she took a turn for the worse. She lingered through the fall, and on the day John Kennedy was assassinated she died. There was so much confusion at the *Times* that although there was a large news item on the obituary page the headline read, DR. EUGENIE WOLLMAN DIES. And someone had misplaced her photograph.

For years and years Lazar kept running into people who had no idea she was dead. When one said, "It can't be true, Genya was going to live to be a hundred," he simply shrugged and couldn't think of anything to say.

Houses

WHEN IT HAD BEEN A NEGLECTED WAREHOUSE NO ONE
had noticed the old Ardsley railroad station; its dirty beige
paint blended into the landscape of road and track and
cattails that had crept west from the river's edge. After
Kate bought the old wreck and had it painted slate blue
with white trim you couldn't miss it. As strangers rode on
the two parkways that ran along either side of Kate's
house, they pointed to the station and wished they could
take time to stop. Old-timers in town regretted that they
had not had Kate Winters's good sense.

At night, especially, Kate felt like a lighthouse keeper.
The constant whirring of the cars was the endless lap of
waves against the rocks. The whistle of the occasional
freight train that ran along the old track, usually at dawn,
was like the foghorn at sea. And Kate knew, as she read far
into the night, that her light was a beacon to lonely drivers
speeding along the parkways.

When her mother died everyone assumed she would
move into an apartment, but Kate surprised herself by
wanting to be utterly alone. She didn't need other people's
lives crowding around her. She had raised three children

and taken care of a sick mother. Now it was time to be by herself. And for once she knew she had done the right thing. As all the vestiges of station and warehouse disappeared, Kate felt that the house and she were starting a new life together. Each day she rose earlier and earlier, brimming with excitement.

The old station had more room than she needed, but it was pleasant to have all that space flowing around the few Shaker pieces that were the only furniture Kate had kept from her mother's house. Against the stark white walls the fine books from her parents' library looked, finally, at home. The large windows were good for Kate's plants; at night lights from the speeding cars leaped across their uncurtained surfaces so the house seemed to sway. Guests found this disconcerting and asked when she was going to get curtains, but Kate liked the illusion. The moving lights gave her a feeling of being in touch with the world again.

The only people who liked Kate's house as well as she did were the two workmen who had transformed it from a railroad station-warehouse to a home. When the Perino brothers first saw the sketches Kate had made, they thought she was crazy. But it was work, they knew she would pay her bills, and she seemed so sure of what she wanted. Then, as they first gutted the station and then rebuilt it, they began to understand.

"That Kate Winters," they told their families, "she knows how to live." Sometimes they would bring their relatives to see their work, and when things were slow the following winter they often stopped in for a visit. The house reminded them of tree houses they had built as boys, when Ardsley was just a rural village — tree houses they and their father had built, one in an oak, and, later, one in a beech tree, where they spent hours on end, dreaming, planning.

Kate loved to see them. It was odd, she thought as she sat with them, that she was so much more comfortable with them than with her friends or her family. Once she said so to Mike, the elder one. "It's because we made something together, Kate." His face reddened.

She smiled. "And it doesn't even talk back."

"How right you are," Mike muttered. Then they would talk about their kids.

"They'll go off to school, find someone, eventually marry. Then it will be easier, you won't feel so responsible," she said. But Mike knew it wasn't so easy, he knew Kate wasn't telling the whole truth.

Mike had met Kate's kids in the spring. Kate was already living in the house although it wasn't completed. Jeremy, the youngest, had stopped one Saturday with his wife and small daughter on their way somewhere else. He had seemed amazed that his mother was able to live there and thought the house was interesting, though not his style. When he left he said, "I do like your overalls, Mother." Kate laughed. She had begun to wear carpenter's overalls during the construction of the house; now she wore them a lot of the time when she was home. "They are a switch from those matching sweaters and skirts," she admitted.

Her daughters hadn't liked anything. "It's so spare, so uncozy," Jennifer, the older one, said. "It looks as if you can't afford more furniture."

And Liz kept worrying that her mother would be attacked or robbed because the house was so isolated. She had gone on and on so long about it that Kate finally said, "Honestly, Liz, I almost think you want me to be raped or robbed." That had shut her up, but there had been a strain at lunch, Mike remembered.

"Our relationship has never been easy," Kate said after they left. "Their father divorced me and married my best friend when they were twelve and fifteen. Jeremy was nine." Kate looked out the window, avoiding their eyes. "They were angry at first. Why couldn't I stay married to their father? they seemed to be saying to me. We stayed in the house for a year after Roy left and we were getting used to living without him, just the four of us; some of their anger was subsiding. But then my mother had a heart attack and asked us to live with her." Kate hesitated. "It was a mistake. She was old, she had gotten more neurotic than I realized since my father died, the kids never felt comfortable living with her in her big house." Kate brushed a lock of hair from her forehead, shrugged. "What's passed is past. I often wish I knew then what I know now."

The two men stared at her as she cleared the table. It had never occurred to them in the six months they had known her that her husband was still alive. She looked like a widow: lined, gray-haired, well provided for. But this? They looked at each other, embarrassed. Kate saw it.

"Now don't you two start feeling sorry for me. That would be terrible!"

Every morning after breakfast Kate walked up to Woodlands Lake and then around it. Growing older without a

job required a schedule; that much Kate knew from having observed her mother and her mother's friends. This
daily walk, which took about an hour, got her out; it gave
her days a structure. The seasons became more real to her.
In spring she tucked *The Trees of North America* into her
pocket and watched the changes on the branches. Her
favorite was a lonely thriving elm. Red-winged blackbirds
skittered along the banks of the lake, flying low, sometimes
knee-high, across her path. With the heat came the purple
loosestrife — heavy, erotic, almost, as it hung over the lake.
As she stopped here and there to watch or listen Kate felt
as she had long ago, when her girls were little. Summers
when she had lived at the shore and Roy had commuted to
the beach house and the sea had been like an interesting
friend. Now this lake was like that. Now she began to
understand why she had been so unhappy living with her
mother and servants and clutter; it was a life so filled with
possessions that there didn't seem time for anything else.
Twenty years of her mother's interfering drone — in her
children's lives and in hers. It had been wasteful, stupid;
she would have been better off if she had had to live on her
own, perhaps even work. Oh, well, try not to rehash, Kate
kept telling herself as she walked around the lake.

One morning late in the summer the telephone rang.
"Mother, did I wake you?"
"No, of course not. I've been out already."
"In this heat?"
"It's not so bad." Kate wished she could tell Liz about
her walk, of her pleasure in watching the ducks' lazy glide
along the shimmering surface of the water, how she loved

the sensual heaviness of the lakefront on hot days. Instead she waited, uncomunicative with her child. An old story.

"It's terrible, Mother. They say it's going to go to a hundred." Liz sounded irritable. "Don and I want you to come to the beach. You'll die in that station with the sun baking on the roof and not a tree around for relief." Kate could almost hear Liz bite her tongue, then resolve to be kinder. "Please come, Mother." Her daughter's voice was softer. "We'd love to have you; it's so beautiful here and the kids have been asking for you."

It wasn't all true, Kate thought. She and Don didn't really know each other; he still fumbled when he had to call her by name. And the kids were a little afraid of her. They had hated coming to her mother's house, and though Kate was sure they would like her new home, Liz wouldn't let the boys visit for a weekend. "It's not safe. There are no neighbors around, Mother," she once said.

But still . . . to go to the sea. She hadn't been there in years. Her mother was allergic to the sun, so while the children used to visit Roy at the beach in the summers she and her mother went to the mountains. Kate closed her eyes. She could see the peculiar grayish ocean blue, her nostrils suddenly filled with the sharp damp smell, she could feel the salt drying on her skin, the sand between her toes. How she would love to go! If they really wanted her.

"I volunteer at the library three times a week," she spoke slowly. "I'll have to check to see if it's okay."

"Oh, Mother, stop being silly. I'm sure they can find someone else."

"Okay," Kate said. "I'll start about three. I should be there by dark."

As she changed her dress, then tidied up her bedroom and the kitchen, Kate thought about presents for the children. She would stop at Big Top on her way home from the library, then pack and have a bite and be on her way.

As Kate walked quickly across the parking lot George Perino came out of the pizzeria.

"Hot enough for you, Kate?"

"I'll say." She smiled. "But I'm going to the beach, to spend some time with Liz and her family. I'm leaving this afternoon."

"Lucky Kate, you always get the breaks! While we're hammering nails, this loafer is going to be sunning herself at the beach!" George greeted Mike as he joined them.

"Hiya, Kate. How long will you be gone?"

"I don't know." Kate realized that she hadn't made any plans. She had been so haphazard. Liz must be sure she was crazy.

"Don't worry, Kate. Stay as long as you can. It's sure hot enough. We'll check the house for you." Kate thanked them.

How pleasant it was to have to hurry. It was twenty-three years since she had seen that particular stretch of beach.

So now Kate sits on the porch of the summer house that used to be hers, that she swore she would never lay eyes on again, rocking her youngest grandchild. It is a peaceful afternoon. The ocean is calm, waves break lazily, ripple slowly toward shore. The jetty glistens, a chameleon under the strong sun. Clouds drift, their undersides rimmed pink, mauve. Kate can feel the sun warming the layers of her skin, thawing the marrow of her bones. She has to be careful not to burn, and day after day (she has been here more than a week) she rubs her arms and legs with oil. She who used to be so brown! Is it possible she has come to this?

Everything is possible. Now, finally, back here again, Kate lets herself follow the path of light in her brain that is the memory. For so many years she has struggled to obscure it. Her life years ago — Roy, her marriage, the children when they were small — seems to have happened to someone else in a silent movie. Even this house had become a papier-mâché backdrop in her mind.

The first time she saw the beach house was surely the hottest day of her life. The sun wanted blood, people barely moved. Slowly she trudged through the burning sand, her feet already swollen in her first pregnancy.

"Where are we going?" she demanded.

Roy smiled and put his arm around her and propelled her a few steps farther. There, behind a bearded dune, was a weathered shingle ranch house with a porch around three sides. The perfect summer house. Her birthday present. For fifteen years she had loved it. Then she gave it away.

"Do you mind, Mother?" Liz had asked when Roy offered the house to her and Don. "Of course not." Kate's voice was brusque. Years before she had signed the house over to Roy as part of the divorce settlement. Kate did mind, though. She had never expected Roy to keep the house after the divorce and come here with Beatrice. Then, when they bought a smaller place a few miles down the road, she thought he would sell it. Instead Roy gave the beach house to Liz.

I am, literally, a guest in my own house, Kate thinks. She stops rocking the carriage. The baby is asleep. The house is absolutely still. Liz and Don and the boys have gone to Montauk for the day. Kate wedges the carriage against the porch railing and walks down the steps and sits on a dune. The house hasn't aged, that's what weathered shingle means. It looks as young as it did the day she first saw it. Her house. Roy's house. Liz's house.

"Why did you go back there? How could you?" The shrill voice attacks her ears.

"Yes, Mama," Kate answers silently. I can see your lips pursed, your hands clasped together to control their old-age tremble. And your voice is high, grating, as it always was when you tried to bully me.

"What have you to say, Kate?"

"What I have to say you won't believe, Mother. I like being here. I'm glad Roy didn't sell the house. He was right. A house like this should be kept in a family."

Smiling, strangely content, Kate turns toward the sea, leans back on her elbows. Some children are playing in the wet sand. From far away they could be her own kids — building, imagining, listening. They never argued here at the beach, and every summer they were so glad to leave her mother's house and come here to visit Roy without her.

Slowly Kate draws her knees up to her chin, as if by crimping her body she can control her thoughts. No use. And you, Roy? He stares at her. What do you think? Old. Kate's gotten old. Her face is a network of anxious lines. But what can you expect, Roy? You can't divorce a woman and marry her best friend without something happening to her. Then bringing up three children and coping with a neurotic mother. And that house! That horrible old house!

Then Kate hears Roy's voice: reasonable, soft. "Let me help you, Kate, please let me help you." But she hadn't listened. Too much pride.

Kate slumps over her knees. One minute no pride, the next minute all pride. And for whom? Imaginary people, in silent conversations. Isn't that what remembering is? Isn't that why she tries to avoid it?

Quickly Kate stands up and walks back to the house. As she reaches the steps the baby cries. Two hours gone like a rustle of wind. She picks up the baby. Her name is Diane. She's very warm, trickles of perspiration run down either side of her plump face. Kate wipes it with a diaper, then rocks Diane on her lap. Back and forth. Back and forth. Soon the crying stops. Kate takes her fat fingers. "This little piggy," she begins. The child grins. Why, she has Roy's smile! Now Kate knows why Liz and Don look at each other whenever she admires the baby. Diane looks like Roy.

"None of my kids look like me," Roy used to tease her. The girls looked like her and Jeremy was exactly like her own father. Yet now this youngest grandchild is like him: the shape of the head, the wide-set eyes, the deep indentation in the upper lip. Roy's face. For eighteen years just the sight of it made her happy. Until those last months when he kept drawing away from her and she so stupid. For months Kate had deluded herself, tried not to see Roy's and Beatrice's need for each other, their eyes, their gestures, and then their concern for her. At the end they had begun to treat her like an invalid.

The day they decided to separate was still, so many years later, a blur in her mind. But she remembered that as he spoke and moved Roy was already a stranger in his own home.

"The children," she had said.

"They'll hate me, but I have to live, too."

Roy was wrong. The girls have always loved him, and if Jeremy isn't that affectionate, well, he's that way with everyone. I should have let Roy and Beatrice bring him up, Kate thinks; he needed a father and he would have had the companionship of Beatrice's sons.

Then, to move in with her mother. Why had she done it? It seems unbelievable to her now: that she had actually packed up three kids and moved out of her house to her mother's. Foolish Kate, everyone said behind her back, a few to her face. And they were right. But they didn't know of her strange mixed feelings when she looked at her children, sometimes blaming them because she had loved them better than their father. She wasn't the best wife; she knew it then, she knows it now. But you don't admit that to anyone. For the year after the divorce she had felt surrounded by her mistakes, wherever she turned she bumped into them. Turning, turning, even in her sleep, so that when her mother had asked Kate to come live with her she said yes.

If she couldn't be a good wife, at least she could be a good daughter. But it had been too much for her. She felt pulled to pieces between her mother and the children; in the end she had failed her children. Gradually, quietly, they had relinquished their positions in that long, silent tug-of-war, and now Kate's children are strangers to her.

Her past is sad, confusing, like lots of people's pasts. But she has survived. The body is a marvelous machine, she learned when she stopped fighting and let it pull her around. And now she has her new house. And today she has this grandchild. Kate holds the baby high. Diane giggles.

"You're a darling baby, but you're very wet," Kate tells her.

Inside it is cool. Simply furnished with many of the pieces Kate chose herself, this house is filled with blues and greens which make the bleached cypress walls appear lighter than they are. The baby's room, once the guest room, is way in the back.

Singing softly, Kate changes the baby. Then she puts her into the playpen in the living room. As she is running a comb through her hair she hears voices. Kate hurries out, afraid Liz and Don will think she's neglecting Diane.

In the hall she stops, too stunned to move. Roy is on his hands and knees talking to Diane. Beatrice has her back to them as she looks out the huge window. The lowering rays of the sun cast a deep pink glow over the room. None of it seems real. Kate leans against the wall, closes her eyes. She hasn't seen either of them for twenty-two years. In all that time, in all those imaginary scenes she has conjured in her mind, they have grown as huge as monsters. But here is Beatrice, still small and slender as she was at thirty-eight. And Roy's skinny frame is like a boy's. They seem so ordinary, so harmless, that her first reaction is relief.

"Hello, Katie." Roy takes her hands. She smiles at the sound of his diminutive for her and at the familiar touch of his knuckly hands.

"Hello, Roy. Hello, Beatrice." Her voice is surprisingly firm. She feels herself looking directly into their eyes. There is an awkward silence. What can they say? They couldn't hope to cover the deaths, the marriages, the births. So they admire the baby, just to talk a little, and Kate realizes that they aren't what she expected. They seem content, and she can't deny a small prick of envy, but with the contentment is also a staidness, a vague weariness that surrounds a lot of couples their age. Lives lived in grooves. Happiness of a sort, but so different from what she feels these days that she is astonished. And relieved. Slowly, almost perceptibly, the jealousy and bitterness she has nurtured for so many years seem to melt. Her body feels light, she could float; for a second she feels faint and gasps as though a draft has gone through her.

"Cold, Kate?" Roy asks.

"No, no, I'm fine. Let me make you a drink."

"Oh, we can't stay, we came back from Maine early and wanted to say a quick hello, but we're having dinner with friends." Kate nods. She knows Liz thought they would be gone till next week.

"Please stay, I'm not angry," she wants to tell them. Instead: "Diane looks like you, Roy."

"Well, it's about time someone in my family did." They laugh at the old joke. It is pleasant to be with them again; she shouldn't have let so many years go by. Now Kate wishes she could give them some sign that she forgives them. Signs. Signs. She was never good at giving signs. So Kate sits and listens to Roy talk about Maine.

Finally Beatrice says, gently, "Tell us about your new house, Kate."

"Oh, it's a marvelous house. The girls aren't crazy about it, I know, but I love it. I like the independence, the light, the closeness to the sky. It's near a lake and I take a long walk every day. I'm learning a lot about the trees and birds and wild flowers. And in the fall I'm going to plant a garden — there's a flat spot on the south end of the land that will be perfect for an English garden."

The words tumble out so fast, Kate chuckles. They look politely puzzled.

Soon they must go. Kate knows it would be useless to try to persuade them to stay for dinner. They are not used to changing plans, that's clear. She walks with them to their car, holds Diane up for them to kiss. Then she watches their old Mercedes disappear around the curve in the road.

With the baby squirming in her arms Kate looks toward the horizon. People are hurrying home, leaving the beach to the gulls and a few loners. This was always her favorite time of day here. Roy's, too. Kate and Roy. Roy and Beatrice. Now that she has seen them once she will see them again, from time to time. But it won't matter anymore.

Much later that evening, after everyone is supposed to be in bed, Kate gets up to make herself some hot milk. She slips on her robe and starts toward the kitchen. Liz and Don are there; helplessly she eavesdrops.

"Poor Mother. Here I thought she and Diane would have a quiet afternoon on the beach and this has to happen," Liz says.

"She's never seen them since the divorce, has she?" Don asks.

"No, when we were growing up we tried to persuade her

to see Daddy. But she always left when he came to visit. It was so difficult then — divorce was much rarer, she was so bitter, we were so ashamed. When Jenny and I were married we both wanted Daddy there, but we couldn't bring ourselves to ask her. You remember that."

Kate feels her heart turn over. She had planned to say yes each time, but they never asked. How sad it was!

Liz's voice is filled with concern. "What a horrible day this must have been. Honestly, Don, she has no luck. Here's she's locked herself in that fortress of a house she bought, cut herself off from the friends she and Grandma had, and then she finally comes back here and this happens. Oh, God, I wonder how she survives!"

"Now wait a minute, Liz. She likes her station house and she seems quite happy. A lot happier than when she was living with your grandmother. And she seems to have new friends, she does volunteer work. Why, even you thought she looked better when she arrived." Kate is touched by his defense.

"Oh, Don, you don't really know Mother. Nobody does, that's the pity. It's hardly a life. A few workmen who like her coffee and the library. I don't know how she manages. Poor Mother . . ."

Poor Mother. Poor Kate. It's been that for so long. And here she is, happier and freer than she has been for years! Kate wishes she could go on the porch and feel the salt hanging in the damp night and rock back and forth with a cigarette or two. But that would only worry them. So, like a good guest, she goes back to her room, climbs into bed, and pretends to be sleeping when Liz opens the door a crack.

A few hours later the whole house is awakened by a terrific thunderstorm, the kind that hits only after a long stretch of extreme heat. While Liz calms Diane and Don hurries through the house fastening down windows and doors, Kate stands in the living room, her arms around her two grandsons. Quietly they watch the snarling ocean; with each flash of lightning the sea gets angrier. The roar of the thunder and the waves seems about to deafen them when, suddenly, the storm stops. They all laugh in relief and go back to bed as the dying wind swirls around the house.

Next morning the phone wakes them.

"Mother." Liz knocks on Kate's door. "It's Mike Perino, something about the house."

Kate hurries to the phone.

"I'm sorry to bother you, Kate, but the storm broke the big bedroom window last night," Mike says.

"Oh, thank goodness it's nothing more."

"Listen, Kate, that's a stock window, and George and I can replace it this afternoon. You won't even know it was broken when you get home."

Home. Suddenly Kate wants to be home. She had planned to stay at the beach for another week, but now she wants to be back at her house. "I'd better come home today," she says firmly into the phone.

"There's no reason for you to cut your vacation short." Mike sounds annoyed.

Kate softens her voice so he will understand. "I'd rather be there, Mike, please."

"Okay, Kate, have it your way. See you later."

Liz frowns when Kate tells her what has happened.

"I think I'd better go home."

"Oh, Mother, I hate to see you go. You were just getting settled in here, you were just beginning to relax." Liz's voice is filled with regret. Kate is almost tempted. But then she feels that pull back to her house. Impulsively she hugs her daughter; Liz is surprised.

"I'll come back again, darling, more than you want me," Kate reassures her. Then Kate smiles and goes to her room to dress and pack.

Debut

I AM STANDING AT THE ENTRANCE TO TULLY HALL. Most of the faces around me are smiling the way people smile when they have no stake in the matter. They are here for pure pleasure. Some of the heads and hands motion toward my wife and me. One figure brushes close to us and says, "This is worse than a wedding!" but he's too young to know anything. Politely I nod. My wife puts her hand on my arm. "Let's go backstage again," she pleads. I have dragged her out here to see the crowd; she hates to be stared at. But I also hate to watch my son. He seems so calm, yet I know that we make him nervous. Especially his mother. She can't seem to keep her hands off him, straightening this, brushing off that, just as she used to when he was a kid getting ready to go to school. As soon as she said, "Don't forget your milk money," he forgot.

I don't want him to forget anything tonight, so I said very quietly to her, "I need some air." Since I have had what looks suspiciously like a small heart attack, she couldn't refuse. Besides, my daughter, Sonya, is here from Columbus, Ohio, with her husband and small daughter. My son adores his older sister; it's better for them to talk together now.

"Come on," I said. "Just for a few minutes." We went outside and I took a few deep breaths, and now we stand here in the lobby on the fringe of all these elegant people who will always be different from us no matter how many new suits I buy.

"Oh, there's Mr. Voronsky." My wife's voice is filled with relief. We wave and he and his wife come over. She is wearing a crushed-velvet cape and looks as if she were born in Tully Hall. As of course she was, in a sense. Who knows how often they come here? I must remember to ask him later how often one of his students plays here.

My wife's hand slips from my arm to my hand; it is clammy and she has that frightened expression she always gets when confronted by a sophisticated woman. My wife is a country girl, my southern belle from Roanoke, Virginia. I met her when I was a salesman in women's dresses, before I got into ladies' sweaters. I loved her in the long, ruffled, off-white dresses she wore. But they never looked the same after we were married and settled in Seagate. We built a house not unlike the one she grew up in, and we even have a porch and a glider like the one we courted on. She says she loves it here, but she's never as happy as she is when we go back to Roanoke to visit her ailing older sister.

We talk with the Voronskys; they introduce us to several people, but it is like peering through a maze. Soon it is time to go in. Mr. Voronsky and his wife go to the box where they always sit, and we walk to the front row. I wish we weren't so close. With nothing between my son and me I am more aware of that invisible string which ties us together. Farther back, with people between us, I might be able to delude myself a little, I might feel more detached.

As we sit down my wife whispers, "I have never seen so

many Orientals in one place before." I nod. Then her eyes open wider. "Have you ever noticed that there are no bald Japanese men? I wonder what they eat?" I smile and shake my bald, white-fringed head. My father had a marvelous head of hair; she thought I would have one too, but people didn't know then that baldness is carried through the mother's genes.

I am congratulating myself that she is distracted and hasn't mentioned going backstage for one last time when she says quickly, "I'm dying of thirst, I must get one last drink of water." She hurries out, and when she rushes back she has Sonya's daughter, Susie, with her. Behind are Sonya and her husband, Peter. They are all smiling.

I stand up and look around.

The hall is crowded. Against the wood walls the people's clothes form pretty patterns of color; if I squint a little, it looks like a kaleidoscope. It's wonderful that the hall is full, it makes such a difference from the stage. Many of the seats have been given away, but many have been bought, and we will probably break even. I know I shouldn't think about the money, and believe me, it doesn't really matter, but it's hard for me to separate money from the rest of life. Not after spending all these years worrying about it.

A nice audience. A mixture of ages and faces: people from Juilliard, my son's friends and their families, his students (for he has begun to do a little teaching) , and, arriving last, because they will never understand that a concert is not a wedding and starts on time, are our relatives. My sisters and brothers and nieces and nephews and their husbands and wives. Quickly they fill the first three rows and whisper apologies to my wife and me and crackle some paper so their mouths will be busy. "That keeps them calmer," my wife once told me a long time ago, when we went to a Rubinstein concert with the whole family on New Year's Day. I never understood that, since how could they be worried about Rubinstein, but now, at last, it makes sense.

"Oh, I love that Bach," my sister Rella stage-whispers as she opens the program. "Sh-sh-sh," the rest of them chorus, and finally there is silence.

I can almost feel the molecules of silence pressing against my temples, and I wonder how many times in my life I have daydreamed this moment. On the living room couch while he practiced, on subways, trains, in the car, later on planes. When I was going through an unfamiliar door to try to open up a new account. When I gave my card to a cold fish of a secretary who made me wait a half hour more than was necessary. And, of course, at other concerts.

We were always going to concerts. Sometimes I yearned for a track meet or a hockey game, and once we played hooky. We were supposed to hear Serkin at Carnegie Hall, but as we passed the new Madison Square Garden, my son said, "Hey, Pop, how about it?" Before we knew it we were sitting in a box watching the Rangers play Montreal and eating popcorn as if we had never tasted it before. Suddenly my son looked at me guiltily. "We forgot to call and turn the tickets in." He is such a good boy, always thinking of someone else. "Someone who bought standing room will take them," I reassured him.

Now my son walks out. Tall, well built, with his mother's wavy chestnut hair. New silver-rimmed glasses for the occasion. An impressive young man. A grown-up person in a tuxedo getting ready to play the piano in Tully Hall in front of hundreds of people, famous musicians, critics from the New York papers. It is too much for the mind to grasp. But for the grace of God, he could be going to play the accordion at some affair in Great Neck. That's what my father used to say when he heard him practice, often for hours at a time. "So much practicing? Believe me, when they're dancing and have a few drinks in them, they won't know if he's playing so good." "Pa, Pa," my wife tried to be gentle. "He's going to play in concerts, in front of a lot of people who are going to pay just to hear him." "She'll always be a southern romantic," my father said under his breath. I wonder what he's thinking now. I wish I could see his face.

My son sits down. I can see some sweat beginning on his upper lip. I wish he weren't so stubborn and would carry a handkerchief with him. But he doesn't like all those usual affectations of pianists; he can't stand watching people mop their brows, he has always been a very private person. But what is he going to do with that perspiration? It will have to go somewhere. I pull out my handkerchief and wipe my face.

He begins, and as I watch his large, capable hands joining him to the piano, I know he is going to be fine. Occasionally, very occasionally, he has a bad day and doesn't really connect with the piano, but you can hear it on the first note. Tonight he is fine. The Bach prelude is beautiful and quiet. He hates to hit his listeners over the head. The boy has taste. I shut my eyes. I can hear my wife's even breathing on one side; finally she has begun to relax.

On the other side is my sister Esther's asthmatic gasp. It gets worse when she's worried, and she will be worried until the last note of the evening is sounded. She is my spinster sister, and she loves my children as if they were her own. I pat her arm. She smiles. Of all her nieces and nephews, my son has always concerned her most. She thinks he's not as healthy as the others because he was born in the car.

Of course we had a hospital nearby. But my wife hates to be obtrusive or give any trouble; she figured that if she stayed home till the last minute it would be easier for everyone. The doctor had warned her that second children sometimes come very fast, but since Sonya had taken her good old time, it never occurred to either of us that the baby might come so soon. Five minutes before we left the house the pains started to come more quickly. I put her into the back seat and pressed on the gas pedal and prayed nothing would happen. Suddenly my wife gave a huge gasp. I finally knew what it felt like to have your hair stand on end. I pulled over and got out, and before I had opened the door I heard a cry. Sometimes when I am walking along the street, or opening the door to see a customer, that cry comes to visit me from nowhere. It becomes an omen in my head, and no matter how late it will make me, I go to the nearest phone and call my son. He's usually not home, so then I call my wife, who is so delighted that I wanted to talk to her that I have never been able to tell her about that cry and its independent life.

When I opened the car door I saw a baby boy, perfectly formed. And little else. It was an unusual birth. The baby seemed to have popped out, without the ordinary mess. At least we had had the sense to grab some clean sheets on our way out of the house. I wrapped the baby in a sheet and put him on my wife's stomach. As we drove the rest of the way I thought he might die because nothing was sterile and it was winter. But my wife wasn't frightened at all. "Look at him, isn't he beautiful?" she kept saying to my numbness. "Look at his hands, such nice long fingers," she kept saying. They were long for a baby and they grew to be short and stubby, the kind the best pianists have. Now they are playing that long slow movement of the Brahms sonata. People are concentrating; it isn't easy music.

In the emergency room, where the doctor cut the cord, I asked over and over again, "Is he okay?" "Of course, he's fine, you just have to look at him to know he's fine," everyone said. His little fists began to beat the air and he cried at the top of his lungs. Then they took the baby and I walked next to one of those stretchers on wheels to the delivery room, where they would deliver the placenta. My wife smiled at me and kept murmuring. "It's a miracle, a miracle." Neither one of us heard the nurse's question, so of course they put down his name as Michael even though we had planned to name him Jonathan after my mother, Jessica, who had recently died.

Michael Lochman. Jonathan Lochman. After all these years Michael is probably better. Less euphonious. Not as studied. Anyway, about six months later my sister Lotte had her first daughter, and named her Joyce.

Applause washes over me. Michael stands and bows. "Bravo, bravo," they call, and I realize I have been so deep in my own thoughts that I hardly heard any of the Brahms sonata. It is a difficult one, rarely played in New York — the one selection on the program Michael felt he had to play for the critics. And I was scarcely aware of it. I clap very hard to cover up my shame. How could I have wandered so far away?

"Brilliant!" My brother-in-law Max shakes my hand.

"He's absolutely marvelous," my niece Rhoda says to her husband.

Sonya hugs me.

Peter shakes my hand.

Esther says mournfully, "Such a hard piece. Make sure he lies down during intermission."

Little Susie pulls at my sleeve and we go backstage together. Michael grabs my hands. Oh, how I used to worry about those hands! He and his cousins rolling around the floor on Sundays. Wrestling, they called it, and whenever they got up it took all my self-control not to ask, "Are you all right, no fingers broken?" And then after he had an apartment of his own, a walk-up no less, with fifteen concrete steps outside. What if he should fall on the icy steps and hurt his hands, or his wrist? I criticized his mother when she harangued about it, but I was just as bad.

Good strong hands.

Michael puts his arm around me and draws me into the dressing room. "Pop, I'd like you to meet a friend of mine, Sandy Lewitt. She works for the *Village Voice*. They would like to do a story on me, a human interest thing. She wants to talk to you for a few minutes."

A skinny, flat-looking girl with lots of beads and straight, dirty-blond hair smiles at me, and I can feel myself being shunted out into the hall when I want to be in the dressing

room with Michael. Now I know we can't make him nervous; once he has gotten this far the rest will go as well,
and I want to share these moments with my family.

"When did you know Michael was going to be so unusual?" she asks. Her voice is high and breathy. I can see
she's perspiring a little, too; maybe this is her first story.

"Unusual how? Musically or otherwise?" I stare.

She thinks I'm crazy, but what she doesn't know is that
Michael won art contests when he was in elementary
school, when he was just another kid taking piano lessons.

She shrugs, then begins again. "When did Michael start
to play the piano?"

"When he was seven."

"Did he want to take lessons?"

"Yes, of course. His sister took lessons and he used to go
to the piano and pick out her pieces by ear."

Her eyes light up; she writes furiously.

"When did you know he was going to be a pianist?" she
asks innocently.

Know? Know what? You don't know anything in this
world, I want to tell her, especially about your kids. You
only hope and pray that they'll have a little luck. But I
must be polite. I shrug.

"I didn't really know till quite late, maybe not until
tonight," I say truthfully.

"Oh, how witty!" she says admiringly.

Suddenly I'm tired. "Can we sit down?" I say, but she
ignores me.

"When did Michael decide he wanted to be a concert
pianist?"

"Listen, my dear girl, I don't think people decide to do

things in such a clear-cut way. One day his teacher said, 'I can't teach him anything more, I think he'd better go to Juilliard.' So he applied and auditioned and got a scholarship and went to Juilliard and studied with Mr. Voronsky."

"He's a very famous teacher, isn't he?" She is so young and eager that under other circumstances I might have wanted to help her, but now she seems a little dumb. I see Voronsky leave the dressing room and think, If I were a nice man, I'd point him out to her, but I don't want her to go bothering him, he's such a busy, famous man.

"The best!" I say in my salesman's voice.

"Mr. Lochman's son, Michael, studies piano at Juilliard with Boris Voronsky," my customers were always telling their customers. In sweaters that's better than marrying a Rockefeller.

As if heaven-sent, the bell rings. My wife suddenly materializes and presses my shirt collar down. It has a habit of creeping out.

"She's cute, isn't she?" she says, but I don't know if she's talking about the *Village Voice* girl, who has just backed away, smiling, or Susie, who is swishing proudly in her long pink dress in front of us. I nod.

"Mr. Voronsky is beaming," my wife reports as we settle ourselves for the second half of the concert. Here Michael is more relaxed than I have ever seen him. He also plays better than I have ever heard him, although some of that must be due to the acoustics of the hall. The audience screams and claps after the Rachmaninoff prelude, but Michael doesn't even wait long enough for their applause to run out. He is already seated for the Debussy. He is so involved in the music that I'm not sure he is hearing much else. His face has that dreamy expression it always has when he is happy.

"What's the rush?" Esther whispers. "He's giving them their money's worth. He barely took an intermission, and now he doesn't even know how to take a little rest between numbers."

"He's young, leave him alone." I touch her elbow. It is bony and old. As Michael plays the Debussy, I am glad he didn't postpone this debut until spring. "It's too cold, the weather might be bad, people don't like to come out in winter," his manager said, but Michael overrode his objections. Who knows what next spring, next month, next week might bring?

Michael's chair begins to squeak at the end of the Debussy.

"Before he plays the encores he should get another chair," my wife says in her "tell him, tell him to do something" voice that I have heard ever since Michael was a year old and developed a mind of his own.

"He knows," I tell her through the clapping at the end. The applause is deafening. The young ones stamp their feet. I look up. Voronsky is standing and clapping.

Then Michael comes out. There is a hush. He bows slightly (he has never had a good bow, it seems to embarrass him) and looks directly at me as if he wants to tell me something. I last saw that look when he was about five and had the croup and couldn't talk and was practically choking. We rushed him into the bathroom and turned on all the taps and sat in the steam, and finally he began to smile and breathe easier. Then I knew we wouldn't have to go to the hospital. It was a look of pure gratitude.

It was beautiful, that long look he gave me in Tully

Hall, but it made me want to look away, and I was relieved when he sat down and played my favorite piece, Chopin's *Raindrop Prelude*. There was a pause when he finished, a long, lovely sigh, then more applause. He played two more encores, a Bartók and, finally, one of Mendelssohn's *Songs Without Words*.

My wife turned to me, her eyes brimming over. She clasped my hand. Sonya kissed me. "Isn't it wonderful," she said in her naturally gay voice, "after all those years!" Then I lost them both and faces began to converge around me. I felt in the middle of a whirlpool. People shouted in my ear, pumped my hand, slapped my back. I tried to put my coat over my arm, and as I did a glove fell out of the pocket, but I knew it would be useless to try to find it now. I would come back later and look for it. People practically pushed me toward the dressing room. Excitement seemed to sparkle like fireworks around me. "What a beginning!" "A success!" "Fantastic!" "Marvelous!" Then I discovered that if I stood still the rest of the crowd would float around me. For some reason I needed to be by myself for a minute. Soon there were very few people left in the auditorium, and I walked slowly back to my seat. I bent down and picked up my glove. As I was straightening up, the little newspaper girl lunged toward me. She came from nowhere.

"Are you okay, Mr. Lochman?" she said with genuine concern in her voice.

I smiled. "Fine, fine, just a little stiff from all the sitting, and I lost my glove . . ." I gestured it was nothing, hoping she would go away. But she had pulled out her pad and pencil.

"Tell me, Mr. Lochman," she said in her official reporter's voice, "how does it feel to be the father of such an astounding success?" She made Michael sound like a sculpture they were unveiling in some city park.

"You must feel wonderful," and added, her eyes shining, before I could answer.

"He's always been a good boy," I said, because if I told her the truth she would never believe me and stay for more and more questions.

The truth was I felt empty — not empty like the seats in the hall around me, which held the promise of another concert, but as empty as the rain barrel that used to stand next to our little house in Europe, as empty as that rain barrel in the terrible year of the drought.

Widow

SHE TAKES A BITE FROM ONE OF THE STRAWBERRIES she has bought, though the snow is waist-high outside. "Did I ever tell you about the dinner I once made for Stokowski? He liked to eat simply, but well, so I made veal cordon bleu, a rice mold and a dandelion leaf salad, with fresh fruit and Brie for dessert. And he slept like a lamb that night."

No one could know if Stokowski ever ate or slept at Millie's. Family consensus: No. Of all her musicians we met only one, a woman pianist named Rae Lev who was fairly well known in the forties. The rest float in and out of her stories, which come in different shapes and sizes. And there's the giveaway. Real events stick like glue in the memory, that's why they get repeated so often.

Today we have been summoned to her apartment. It is almost unrecognizable. Her precious photographs are packed away; her fancy table is set with paper plates; we are all, the four sisters, moving to Sarasota tomorrow.

"Finish the mango!" she orders, and we do (the refrigerator must be empty).

She begins: "Everyone in Florida is a widow. No?"

Frances nods, having firsthand knowledge of that category.

"Unless your husband is still alive," Jenny says, looks in my direction. That takes care of us.

"Of course," Millie says impatiently.

"And there may be some women-who-have-never-married," I venture.

"Exactly! Spinsters." She alone can say the dread word. Then she wets her lips; her voice is pure honey. "That's why I asked you here today. I am changing my abode, and," she hesitates, "I am also changing my marital state. I am becoming a widow."

Jenny and Frances look at me. "And who, may I ask, is the lucky man? Pierre Monteux or Bruno Walter?"

The other two smile.

"Neither."

"Then maybe Mischa Elman?" She met him once when she was young.

"Of course not. Have you no imagination? Come, Jenny, surely you can guess." Jenny is the eldest. She shakes her sensible white head. She believes in her heart that Millie is crazy; she keeps looking for signs of it in the children and grandchildren, but so far we've been lucky.

"Mottel." The name rolls off Millie's tongue. "Mottel Schneiderman. Don't you remember, Jenny? He played the piano like Horowitz and Rubinstein combined." Jenny shrugs.

"So what happened to him?" I expect a famous name.

"He died, in twenty, fighting General Denikin and the Whites."

"You were seventeen then," Frances says.

"And I have loved him for over fifty years."

"But you were only seventeen," Frances protests. "And we didn't even know him."

"Women married younger then. And I knew him. That's all that matters. We were married secretly for three months, then he went away to fight."

"And your name is really Natasha," Jenny mumbles, but Millie is hard of hearing on that side.

"So are you Millie Schneiderman or Millie Brand?"

"It was a secret marriage, I just told you that," Millie says. No one says anything. Then I get up.

"Okay, darling, from now on you are a widow." I kiss her, wondering how I'm going to explain this to Abe and the children and their kids. "And maybe," I add as she hands us our coats, "after all these years you'll remarry."

"Who knows?" Her voice is merry, authoritative again. "That, my dear sisters, is in the hands of God."

Golden Village is divided into sections of eight garden apartments each. "Clusters," the real estate agent called them when he came to New York to show us colored slides of various communities in western Florida. Each sister has an apartment in a different cluster. Abe and I are in the De Soto, Jenny and Walt are in the Vasco da Gama, Frances has the best apartment in the Cortez, and Millie is, of course, in the Ponce de León. Her apartment overlooks a lush garden with a fake fountain of youth that has quickly become the busiest birdbath in Golden Village.

Settling in took time and wasn't easy. For any of us. The constant sunshine had a strange effect. A lot of our activities in New York depended on the weather, and often our most interesting days over the years were spent in museums or galleries or at concerts when it rained. After a few weeks in Sarasota we were tired of being outdoors all day. But soon Frances found a hospital; now she's in charge of the pediatric volunteers and has a new macaroni necklace every day. Jenny discovered a group of potters and sculptors; she goes off in her rags three mornings a week and comes home happy. I work at the library and have become active in the Friends of the Symphony Orchestra. Abe and Walt play a lot of golf and bridge and go to woodworking and gardening classes together.

Only Millie isn't quite herself. I tried to get her involved in the symphony, and she joined, but she doesn't want to be active. Her apartment is the most artistic of any in her cluster, or in the entire Village, but now that it's fixed up she doesn't seem to know what to do with herself.

"She doesn't seem comfortable here," Jenny said the other day. Jenny uses the word "comfortable" the way other people use "happy." No one has a right to be happy in Jenny's eyes; happiness is simply an American delusion. But to be comfortable is different; that is everyone's right.

"What would make her more comfortable?" Jenny had stopped off on her way home from her class; her face was smudged with clay; she was clearly worried.

"Who?" Abe had just walked in.

"Millie. Who else?"

"Oh, Millie misses New York; she liked the noise, the activity, even the dirt. She was always getting something in her eye and she never complained. It's too quiet here, but she'll get used to it," he said as he washed his hands at the kitchen sink, then sat down to his farmer cheese and vegetables.

Abe is right. Millie's favorite place in New York is Chinatown. She went down there two, sometimes three, times a week to shop for vegetables. Lots of shopkeepers knew her. "Hello, missus," they said, and smiled.

Suddenly Jenny looked at me. It had come to both of us at once.

"Cooking!" she said.

"Millie can teach a course in Chinese cooking!" I almost shouted.

"And where do you think I can buy the vegetables I would need to teach Chinese cooking?" Millie looked at us disdainfully later that afternoon. She was stringing a necklace of shells she had gathered on the beach.

"There are no Chinese food stores here?" Frances said timidly. We didn't want to irritate Millie.

"None."

"How about mail order?" I said. "Abe gets beautiful wild flower plants by mail; they pack everything so much better these days." That she didn't even bother to answer.

There was an awkward pause. Finally Jenny asked, "Where do the Chinese restaurants get their vegetables?"

"Who knows?" Millie's shoulders began to slump. I ran to the phone and called the nearest Chinese restaurant. A charming American voice answered. She told me that they ordered things from New York and they came in wonderful condition — airmail.

I came back to the living room triumphant. "I'm sure they'll order for you, too."

"Now why would a Chinese restaurant want to help someone who was going to take business away from them?" Millie said.

"I don't know, but I'll convince them," I answered grimly.

That night Abe and I went to the restaurant and explained what Millie wanted to do. The owner was delighted. He thought it would stimulate business to have Chinese cooking classes. He promised us he would order whatever Millie wanted, and he also gave us the names of the best wholesale fish suppliers. "Sarasota is a wonderful place for seafood; what a good idea you have!" he said. On top of that he wouldn't let us pay for the meal.

Abe got nervous. "What does he want?"

"Nothing. He's just a nice man. Haven't you ever met a nice man?" I answered irritably, hoping I was right.

It turned out that the Chinese restaurant owner was one of the rare good men of this world. A true gentleman. Without any explanations he seemed to understand how important this was to Millie and the rest of us, and he was as cooperative as he could be. We advertised in the local papers, invested in about a dozen woks, and prayed. Eighteen people signed up for Millie's weekly classes.

They were astonished that you could cook Chinese food without a lot of MSG, they were delighted that a Chinese meal high in protein and low in calories could be so reasonable.

Millie was constantly busy — planning her classes, ordering her vegetables, answering questions on the phone, going to dinner at her students' homes. She didn't even have time to miss New York. Besides, she was developing a shell necklace business, too. She did that in the evening while she watched television, and one of the fancy boutiques in Palm Beach had asked her for some of her things on consignment.

Millie's cooking classes changed my life a little; Jenny's, too. Abe and Walt had volunteered to go to the fish markets once a week for Millie, so every Tuesday we rose at 4 A.M. and got the men breakfast so they could get the best choices. And when the children came down to visit us over Easter vacation they were all overweight on their baggage, which was filled with hairy melons, *bok choy,* Chinese leeks, cabbage and okra. But they didn't mind. "Aunt Millie looks terrific," they said, practically in unison. The rest of us sighed in relief. We were home free until the summer.

On June 15 everything in southern Florida seems to stop. A lot of people go north to visit their children and get away from the humidity; the ones who can't afford to leave move very slowly from their air-conditioning to the Gulf of Mexico and back again. Cooking is minimal, so Millie's classes were finished until the fall.

Naturally we assumed that Millie would come north with us when the time came. There were lots of empty rooms in our children's houses; most of the grandchildren went to camp. We had already heard from Adrienne, Frances's older daughter. "I redecorated Lisa's room last spring, and Aunt Millie will love it," that dear child wrote. "We expect her for the summer."

"No," Millie said firmly. "I'm too old for flowered dust ruffles. I want to stay in my own home."

We couldn't believe it. "Does she want to be coaxed?" I asked Abe.

"Coax her," he replied. I tried. She wouldn't budge.

Walt talked to her one night when the six of us went out to dinner. "Is it the money?" he asked gently, knowing very well it wasn't. Millie had made a good living working for a large entertainment agency in New York.

"Of course not," she said brusquely, then she relaxed a little.

"Look, *kindaloch*." We were standing in a circle on the main street. "It has taken me almost six months to get used to this place. Now I'm comfortable. Let me stay here if I want to." She sounded so reasonable that the subject was dropped.

"She'll change her mind when the heat comes," Walt said. But he was wrong. We left and we wrote to Millie and we called her every Friday night. She sounded calm and happy.

What fools we were not to have guessed the truth! Now that I think about it, I'm embarrassed that it took us so long to realize what was happening.

Millie had a boyfriend. She had met him early in May. His name was Isaac Robbins. He had a high cholesterol count so he had sent his cook from St. Petersburg to Sarasota to take Millie's Chinese cooking lessons. They had invited Millie for dinner; that's how it began. He and Millie had seen each other every day during the summer, we learned from the gossips who had watched them.

"Why didn't you tell us?" I asked Millie.

"I'm entitled to some privacy," she answered.

Isaac is a small, well-made man of almost eighty. "Fine," our mother would have called him if he had come to court Millie fifty years ago. He has children and grown grandchildren; he is American-born and so were his parents. He graduated from MIT in 1918 with a degree in chemical engineering, but has been involved in the family business all his life. No one seems to know how the family made its money — some people say banking, one man we know in West Palm Beach says submarines, another man says copper wire.

When we met him Isaac told us, "Millie and I have so much in common. Both our first spouses were musicians. Mottel was a pianist, and my wife Marion was a violinist. A beautiful violinist. She played chamber music every week of her adult life, except when we were traveling."

"How lucky she was," Millie said with a sigh that day. "Mottel could have been another Horowitz. Poor boy, nipped in the bud before his career could begin."

I guess Millie talks to Isaac about Mottel now and then. But it was so long ago. Even love fades with age. Besides, who can dwell on the past when so much is happening in the present?

The wedding took place on Millie's birthday in December. It was one of the most beautiful days of my life. Millie was radiant, happier than we have ever seen her. When he danced with me, Isaac said, "A second wedding can never be like the first, but I tried."

His cousin took my hand as we walked out of the ladies' room together. "It's hard for people who have been happily married to be alone again. Millie had such a good life with Mottel, and Isaac adored Marion, and now look" — she gestured toward them dancing together — "now they have each other. It's like a miracle."

They are very happy. Millie still teaches Chinese cooking; now their cook goes to the fish market. She also has two classes; so many widows heard about her good luck that the registration doubled. She rents a room at the local Y and teaches all Tuesday afternoon. At first Abe and I and Jenny and Walt were glad not to have to get up early once a week, but recently the men have been talking about helping Millie again. They miss the fish market. And now we have a huge vegetable garden between the De Soto and the Vasco da Gama. We've planted the borders with flowers (to keep the owners of Golden Village happy), but the bulk of the garden is Chinese vegetables. They like the cool weather, so we have been eating snow peas and black beans and Chinese cabbage all winter.

Millie and Isaac also travel a lot. For their honeymoon they went on a dig in Israel, and every few weeks they spend a long weekend in New York for theater and concerts and the opera, and Chinatown. Isaac loves music. As we get to know him better we realize that he has helped many of the most famous musicians. Their living room in the house in St. Petersburg is filled with signed photographs of Monteux, Serkin and his wife and father-in-law, Adolf Alexander Schneider, Artur Rubinstein, Isaac Stern, Busch. The last time we were there for dinner Abe beckoned to me from across the room. He was standing in front of a photograph of a man who looked familiar.

"Who is it?" I asked.

He turned the photo over. On the back it read: "To my dear friends. Best wishes, Leopold Stokowski." As we stood there, Millie came up behind us and put her arms around us both. "We saw him the last time we went to New York," she said in a gentle, musing voice we hear more and more often these days. "And he's still an incredible man."

A
Bad Baby

SCORCHED LEAVES CLUTTER THE LAWN. WHEN THE dog runs, she leaves a flurry of dust in her wake. Of all the annuals only the smallest, the Thumbelinas, survive.

She sits reading, her head propped on her hand, her feet curled under the shapeless print dress. Her face is still thin; as she grows older her cheekbones become more prominent; tonight the tanned skin across them glows under the light. She feels me watching her and looks up.

I shrug. She is two weeks past her due date.

Later we listen hopefully as a drizzle becomes a downpour.

Early the next morning our child is born.

I walk down the corridor holding a bunch of flowers. I stop for a moment before she can see me. Although it's only seven hours since the baby came — too fast for any anesthesia — and more than twenty-four since she has slept, she looks beautiful. Her hair is curly because of the damp heat, her face is filled with worry and fear, but she has propped herself up and is trying to read. I want to cry at her courage; instead, I force my face into a smile and enter the room.

"Your flowers, madam." I put them down with a flourish.

"Beautiful," she says softly.

"The paper." I start to hand it to her, and she extends her arms. Our baby, a second girl, is very sick. The arteries and veins in and out of her heart are hopelessly twisted, and not a thing can be done to help her.

"I feel as if I've been shot," she says after we have watched the baby gasping for breath in the incubator.

The telephone doesn't stop ringing.

"How's the baby?"

"No good. She can't survive."

"We'll pray."

"Pray? Pray? Pray for what?" she demands angrily.

Days pass. People persist.

"Can't they do anything? Surgery, or . . ."

"No, it's hopeless. We have to wait," she answers in a dull voice I have never heard before.

"Can't they understand?" she pleads with me. "They act as if she has a cold. They keep talking about God. God damn God!" she shouts.

"Where there is life there is hope," her father says.

"No, Dad. The baby's going to die, and there's nothing we can do. We have to wait." She treats him like a child.

Neighbors come with banana cake, applesauce, stewed fruit, plants. "God will help," they tell her while I'm at work.

"Maybe your God helps, but my God stinks." She laughs in their faces. They make excuses for her because she's upset.

Her sister calls, long distance. "Worse things could happen," her sister says. My wife hands me the phone, tears in her eyes. We could have had an invalid child or a Mongoloid, there are still women who die in childbirth, our four-year-old Judy could have been run over by a car, I could have had a heart attack at thirty. We have heard them all.

"When I'm waking up there's a glorious second when I don't remember. Then I do and I'm on a desert, walking, walking," she admits one evening as she bends over her knitting. The baby is almost two weeks old.

"You know, they didn't know where to put me," she says. "They thought I was asleep when we left the delivery room. First they took me to Maternity. 'She had a bad baby,' they said. 'Not here,' the nurse answered. Then they tried Gynecology. 'A bad baby.' 'Not here, we have our hands full,' they said."

They finally put her in Orthopedics.

"Why didn't you open your eyes to stop them?"

"I don't know. I think I wanted to find out what was wrong. They never said. They kept using that same expression, over and over. How can a baby be bad?"

"I don't know."

"The baby came," Judy tells a visitor. "But she's very sick. Sometimes babies are sick." Then she says, "Mommy, why does a baby come out sick?"

"I don't know, darling, but sometimes it happens."

That evening, after Judy is asleep, she says, "I guess the minute you ask why it happens to us, you're dead."

"That's right." The geneticists say it looks like a fluke.
"But maybe there's something in the sins of the fathers,"
she says. "Maybe I was too arrogant. It never even occurred
to me that this baby wouldn't be exactly like Judy. About
a week before the end, I said, 'All I want is for this baby to
come out.' "

"You were exhausted," I say, but she isn't satisfied. I go
on. "It's medieval to talk about the sins of the fathers.
Unless" — I smile at her — "you're more of a believer than
you think you are."

"Don't tease me now," she pleads.

The phone rings less. The ones who couldn't call at first
are embarrassed by now, a month later. Only our parents,
our close friends, our pediatrician bother.

I pick up the extension in the cellar. It's the hospital. I'd
like to protect her, but I know this is one conversation she
has to have on her own. It's the ward resident. I listen.

"You know what's wrong?" he says.

"We're planning to go over the reports with our pediatrician this week."

"That's probably best, since he knows you."

"Is she still on oxygen?"

"No. And she's being fed by a tube instead of intra-
venously."

"I see." She sounds very controlled.

"When are you coming in to see her?" he asks.

"I'm not coming in. I can't," she says.

There is a pause. Then he says, "I know what a sick
child is, because my brother is retarded and I saw what my
mother went through."

"Your mother went through a lot more than I'm going through," she says gently.

But he can't stop. "And you have a well baby at home. Still, it's unusual for the mother not to come. You know, the baby isn't a monster; she looks like the others."

"I know," she says. "She looks a lot like her sister."

He starts to say good-bye, but now she isn't afraid of him. "Doctor, how long will she last?"

"Hard to know — days, weeks, maybe months."

"And the tests are completed?"

"Yes."

"Well, then, what point is there in continuing this —"

He interrupts her. "You're talking about euthanasia. We are morally and medically committed against it, and as long as I have anything to do with this ward there'll be no such thing." It is his set speech.

"I can't come in," she says wearily and hangs up.

"I was listening," I say as I run up the stairs.

"I know. Don't yell at me. I had to ask."

"I'm not angry." I pull her to me. She's trembling.

"The talk about the wonders of modern medicine. You can have it. All I can think of is that baby fighting for every breath. We eat and we sleep and we talk to each other and we laugh and try to make things normal for Judy, and all the time the baby is gasping for breath and no one does anything. And to call and ask why I haven't come in. They're crazy."

I wipe her tear-stained face. "You can't ask them to risk their jobs. You call it mercy, but the law calls it murder. As for visiting the baby, he probably hasn't any children. If he did, he'd understand."

She listens, her face wearing that beaten look I have seen on Judy's face when her friends have been mean to her.

"You're right. You're right. You're always right!" she says as she runs from the room.

Weeks later, she polishes a silver bowl that was a wedding present from close friends. We're having company; the table is set, the house smells marvelous. She's so absorbed in the polishing that for a moment I think she's forgetting. She looks up and smiles.

"You know, I once read that it's better to attach yourself to objects than to people. That's right. Things last, you know where you stand, you can see and touch them. No future in people."

"Now, that's not so," I interrupt her, hating to see her still so bitter. The baby may last as long as a year, the pediatrician told us this week.

"No, not really, but I understand it now, and when I read it I don't think I did."

Days pass. Crisp, cool, shorter than they were. Tomorrow the baby must be moved. The hospital doesn't want her anymore; we have to move her to a nursing home. We sit over uneaten food.

"It's a Kafka novel," she says.

It will be too much for her to hold the baby. I'll go with my father. Somehow this is something you do with your father.

Later she packs the kimonos and receiving blankets she has saved from Judy. I beg her to go to bed. She shakes her head and continues with the careful, tender folding.

She's waiting when I come back.

"Are you all right?"

"I'm fine."

"Were they" — she hesitates — "were they nice?"

"Very. And efficient. We were out in half an hour."

She relaxes a little. Then, knowing I shouldn't but strangely compelled to, I add, "The nurse who dressed the baby kissed her."

She begins to do some of the things she has wanted to do. While Judy is at nursery school she paints. The Russian books are back on her desk, and in the evening when she is tired she practices Schubert Impromptus at the piano. She can't do things halfway. Once, when we were seniors in college, I brought her to a party very late because she was working on a philosophy paper. My roommate greeted her, "Why are you killing yourself? In ten years none of this will matter."

She smiled and shook her head.

Later he confided, "You're nuts if you marry her. She cares too much."

I can't imagine what life would be like not married to her.

"How long does it take to adopt a baby?"

I don't answer.

"You aren't interested, are you?" If you're not interested you should be, her voice is saying to me.

"I can't think about it while the baby is alive."

"But this could last months longer, and I keep thinking it would be so much easier if we had a baby in the house."

"Maybe it would, but let's go through this. Then we'll think about another baby." The words seem to be stuck in my throat before they can come out. My whole body feels stiff.

"We have a lot to offer a child," she says.

Finally she's made me angry. Why won't she leave me alone? Why can't she be content with what she has?

"Why can't you be happy with one child? There are lots of happy families with one child." I'm almost shouting.

She nods, her lips trembling. She hates this as much as I do. Since the baby's birth we have been so gentle with each other.

"That's true," she says in a more normal tone of voice, "and the genius statistic for only children is very high." She shrugs and rubs her palms nervously. "I have a thing about this," she says, "but I think it's wrong to have one child, and I keep trying to figure out if and when."

I grab her hands. "When are you going to stop planning?"

"When I'm dead."

I dig holes and she and Judy toss the bulbs in, straighten them, and cover them with bone meal and earth. It's a wonderful game.

"When will they come up, Mommy?" Judy asks.

"In the spring, sweetheart, when it begins to get warm." The words come slowly. She's wondering what we'll be doing — whether the baby will still be alive, what the doctors will tell us, whether we'll decide to adopt.

"Then the baby will be home." The child's pleased voice jars us. We look at each other.

"No, sweetie, I don't think so," I hear myself saying. "We don't know if the baby will ever come home."

Judy winces. My wife hugs her. "Cry, darling, it will make you feel better," she says.

Judy shakes her head. "What happened to the baby?" she asks.

I kneel and look into her large brown eyes. "Nothing. It's just that she's very sick and one of these days she'll go to sleep forever."

"Does sleep forever mean die?"

"Yes, sleep forever means die."

Every Saturday morning we go ice-skating. The tassels on their matching hats bob as they glide toward me, their eyes shining, their color high from the cold. She looks marvelous.

While she makes lunch, my glance strays from the paper. She looks across the counter at me. Judy is changing her clothes.

"You know," she says, her face suddenly troubled, "there are days when I think it would be a relief to rend our clothes and walk around with ashes on our heads — when I want no part of my sanity, when I don't want to function at all. And there are other times, like today, when I want to skate, and make lunch and laugh, even though . . ." She pauses, for she rarely mentions the baby anymore and doesn't want Judy to hear her. "Even though the baby goes on trying to live. It's scary to be so sane."

The snow dirties, runs down the hills to make wonderful puddles for the kids, troublesome wet spots in cellars for the parents. People we haven't seen for months gather in the road.

"I surely expected to see you pregnant again," one woman says.

My wife backs away. "The baby's still alive," she says.

"Really?"

"Yes." She shrugs and bends down next to where I am looking for crocus shoots.

One woman lingers. "Maybe you could adopt," she says kindly.

"Maybe, someday." I smile and we go back into the protection of our home.

It's a wet, muggy Friday in April. I am home early. As I walk across the back porch, I see that an old friend is here with her children. My wife looks up in surprise, but there isn't even a moment's bewilderment, which would be a sign she was forgetting the baby. Over the past months the baby's struggle to breathe has tormented her. "The pediatrician called me at the office," I say; and she knows the baby is dead.

"Let me come with you," she begs as I change my clothes. The baby must be taken from the nursing home back to the hospital, where they will perform the autopsy. "Please."

"No."

"But now it's different. She's dead. Please." For a moment I weaken. Then I ask myself, How long will it take her to forget the sight of her baby dead? I shake my head. She follows me, pleading, crying, but I don't dare touch her, for then she'll know how much I need her. I can't let her come with me.

I pull out the car. "Please!" she shouts.

"No!" My voice is harsher than I intended, and I flee from her eyes.

"Thank God, God has been good, it's a blessing, everything is for the best." There is a regular chorus of it when word gets around that the baby has died. She is amazed. "What's this God they keep talking about?" She laughs, but her laugh isn't as bitter as it was. The absurdity of their belief has finally amused her.

"The truth is the best," our kind pediatrician advises us, and so we tell Judy. We thought she had understood when we told her the baby wasn't coming home. But this shocks her.

"I thought you had to be old to die," she says.

"Or very, very sick," her mother adds.

"But how can a baby come out sick?" she says. We're too weary to answer right away.

"How can a baby come out sick?" she says again.

My wife tries. "It happens. And each time it happens the doctors learn more, so that maybe it won't happen again."

But Judy isn't interested in any explanations.

"I don't understand," she says as she stands up and then goes out to play.

part
three

Wedding
Day

THE SPIDER DROPS, THEN CLIMBS AGAIN, HIGH INTO
the corner, then drops once more. Fascinated, I stop polishing my nails to watch the intricate process of making a web.
I begin to hum; I once read that spiders have ears in their
legs and like music. On one of her trips through the breakfast room my mother looks at me oddly. I want to grab her
elbow and point to the web, but she will feel obligated to
brush the fragile wonder down. This is no day to admire
a spider's handiwork. Everything must be clean, shining.

I go back to my nails. I'm like a slow-motion movie. My
mother noticed it after breakfast and each time she passes
she mentions the heat. It isn't the heat, although it's ninety-
two degrees at one o'clock. It's me. I'm a little lonely and
that makes me tired and I can't hide it from her.

"I wish you would go to the beauty parlor," she said.
But I have always done my own hair; the shampoo hurts
when they dig their fingers into your scalp; the dryer gives
me a headache. She knows all this but she wants me to be
fussed over.

Instead I sit here, in everyone's way.

I cap the polish, holding it gingerly as I walk through
the kitchen. Jean, our cleaning lady, says, "I thought you

were on the porch with a book." That's where I've been for the last fifteen years. "If you go there and rest I'll bring you some lunch," she bribes me.

"And after you eat I want you to take a nap," Jean says and puts down the tray. She's known me since I was six years old; she doesn't approve of the rings under my eyes — she thinks graduating from college is enough excitement for one month. If I were hers, she told my mother, I would rest for the summer and get married in the fall. My mother no longer listens to Jean, but she knows Jean is disappointed that we aren't having a big wedding. The eldest daughter. Jean can't understand it. Sometimes, neither can my mother, I realize, as I watch the deepening frown between her eyes.

Lunch is a cold meat loaf sandwich, milk, half a cantaloupe. I feel odd having Jean wait on me. She never has before. I smile at her, but she's embarrassed and leaves quickly.

I'm in exile, I think ridiculously as tears climb the ducts up to my eyes. I consider calling Phil, but we have spoken to each other three times already this morning. I put down the sandwich uneaten and try the cantaloupe. It doesn't taste right.

The car flies into the driveway. My younger sisters Barbara and Erica come in carrying cigarettes, cocktail napkins, club soda — the things my mother always forgets.

"Well, well, if it isn't the birthday girl." Barbara is amused to see such a formal lunch. "Jean's work," she says. Erica nods.

"Sit down, ladies." I gesture grandly with a sweep of the hand. They drop wearily into the overstuffed chairs. I hand them each half a sandwich, they share the milk.

"Why did you have to decide to get married on the hottest day of the year?" Erica says. I shrug. They laugh.

Suddenly there's a crash. We go through the kitchen where Jean stares at us as if we were spies and then into the living room. Mother is directing two men who have enormous wire frames in their arms. On these will go the flowers for the bridal canopy, the *chupa*. It's huge. Even bigger than Mother anticipated, I can see, for she is beginning to chew the inside of her lower lip.

"There, that's fine," she says triumphantly as they hang the frame above the mantel. I move closer. My hair is in a ponytail and I'm wearing shorts. One of the men says, "Watch out, girlie."

"That's the bride," my mother announces coldly.

"How about some lunch, Mom?" I want to do something for her. Way back in her hazel eyes I see she's lonely, too. Because we're having such a small wedding we decided to have it on a Thursday. Maybe it was a mistake. If we had gotten married on a Sunday my father would have been around all day.

"Okay." She's pleasing me. I've been hard to please these days, but there has been so much talk, so much arranging.

In the kitchen Jean is annoyed. Mother wouldn't eat for her. I take a tray to my mother and we watch the men place white camellias into the wire frames. It will be a very beautiful *chupa*. And the house looks lovely — just painted and with new lush green carpeting.

"Now, darling, what else must we do?" My mother smiles.

"Not a thing, Mom, you did it all for me." I kiss her lightly, thinking of all the times she got me ready to go to camp, to college, to Europe. How many nights did she stay up hemming and packing, pretending she couldn't sleep?

"Okay, then, you do me a favor." She is bargaining now. "Please go up and take a nap."

I stare at her. Will no one understand that I cannot lie alone today in the room that Barbara and I have shared for more than fifteen years?

"I'll go to the porch and read," I tell her. She nods, preoccupied again, for the caterer has just arrived. The wedding must be catered because my grandparents insist on kosher food and my mother has never kept a kosher home. So everything will be done according to the silly, thousands-of-years-old rules. We will even have ice cream made without milk, a miracle of the modern world, the caterer has assured us.

It wasn't fair to my parents to have a small wedding. I knew it when we talked about it last winter. It snowed that Sunday. When my father came home with the *Times* and the Bialystok rolls there was mist on his thick gray eyebrows and moustache; he hunched his shoulders and rubbed his hands, glad to be in the warm house. Phil came over for breakfast and he told them what we wanted.

There were no interruptions, which is a sign of trouble in our house, but I was too busy agreeing with Phil to notice. When he finished my mother asked if we wouldn't like to have a small chapel wedding and invite our friends. That appealed to me, but Phil shook his head firmly; the immediate family at home was all he wanted.

Naturally, he forgot about the *minyan*. So, in addition to our parents, grandparents and sisters we are expecting my Aunt Helen and Uncle Nat (my mother's oldest sister and her husband) and Ruth and Max, my parents' closest friends.

"I never realized there would be such a fuss," I say to Erica when she walks through the porch.

"A wedding's a wedding," she says.

I pick up *Life*. Elsa Maxwell had a party, Yale's graduation was spectacular, dolphins are more intelligent than we are, Nero wasn't such a bad guy. This is just my speed now. I remember how my eyes ached two weeks ago while taking comprehensives. *The Magic Mountain* is upstairs on my night table but I haven't opened it.

I'll go for a walk. I plow through the dining room. I have the sense to know I should tell my mother. If she misses me today she will worry, as if I were two years old with an itchy foot and apt to be snatched by a kidnapper.

"I'm going for a walk," I tell her.

Sweat buds on her upper lip. I guess I look a little disheveled to be wandering around outside, although I've taken walks looking much worse before. But today is different, and though she is much too kind to say so I understand. I don't look like a bride!

"Okay, Mom, I'll help Barbara." Barbara is upstairs with a portable phonograph. She is trying to find the band on a record of popular classics that plays "Here Comes the Bride." Erica is in the shower. It's four-thirty; the wedding is set for seven.

"Hi, kiddly," Barbara says. By now she is convinced, her eyes tell me, that none of it is real; we are having a "play," just as we used to when we were children.

"We should have gone to a justice of the peace," I say.

"Uh-uh." She wags a finger at me. "Not at all kosher.

Not even Jewish, and you would have had to have all this anyway, to keep Grandpa happy."

Grandpa is my father's father. He is an Orthodox rabbi who no longer has a pulpit in Borough Park, who reads all day long and publishes an occasional article in the Orthodox rabbinical literature. He is learned. And stubborn. And shrewd. Years and years ago he discovered the stock market and made a lot of money — how, no one knows.

Lately he has been crochety and so has my grandmother, but they are eighty-one and age gives them privileges they don't deserve. Besides, my father is a devoted son and I am the eldest grandchild in America, so this time we are letting them have their way.

Mother steps lightly into the upstairs den. She looks at the three of us sitting there and finally she is content. "Are you all packed?" she asks redundantly. She closed my suitcases this morning. I nod.

The phone rings. We hear Jean begin the usual "She's terribly busy . . ." but it is the rabbi who is to marry us (with Grandpa also officiating, of course) . Mother goes to her room and picks up the phone. I follow her and sit on the love seat, now frayed along the arms. I pull a loose thread and think of all the hours I have sat here, straining my eyes as I read in fading daylight.

Suddenly Mother's face is distorted with pain.

"George Bernstein had a heart attack this afternoon and just died," she says softly as she puts the telephone down. George is an old friend; he knew my father when they were young refugees on the East Side learning English at night at P.S. 6. He was here last night to play chess with Dad; later we had coffee and cake with him. He kissed me

and wished me well, and before he left he pressed an envelope, which I still have not opened, into my hand. He was
a dear man.

"The rabbi's at his house. Sylvia's very upset and the
boys are flying home. The rabbi wants to stay there until
the last minute, so I must call him when we're ready." My
mother sits there, stunned, and I wonder what her faith
tells her now. She believes unequivocally in God, which is
more than my father and sisters and I do. I start to say, "If
there's a God, why . . ." but she turns to me, her face
gray.

"Not today, darling, please, not today." Then she cries
tearlessly. I bring her a damp washcloth which she puts
across her forehead as she lies down on the bed. Barbara
goes to pick my father up at the station. I sit with my
mother until he arrives.

Some of my friends are getting engaged, two are married
and shopping for furniture, one just had a baby. My parents' friends are making weddings, watching over the
births of grandchildren, and dying. I remember an old
record player in my other grandmother's house; it had an
enormous handle, and if we were good we could crank it.
Round and round we turned and the music happened on
our ears. Who cranks that bigger handle, I wonder as I
gather my things to go take a shower.

After the hot water I turn on the cold. It clears my head
a little, and when I step out of the shower I feel better.
Just as I pull on a robe my father comes in. Without
knocking, of course — such formalities are unheard of in
our house — but instead of becoming annoyed I kiss him
on the nose. He wants to shave and Barbara is using their

bathroom. Mother is downstairs arranging porch furniture. He takes out his new electric razor and begins the process I have watched so often in awe. I smile and wave to him, for he can't hear me. The old manual razor was so much more civilized, but he can't resist gadgets.

When I next see him he is in his underwear, polishing his shoes in the hall near the linen closet. He always waits until the last minute to polish his shoes. The bald spot on top of his head glistens. He seems determined to treat this afternoon like any other.

"So?" he says tentatively.

"So?" I reply.

"So." Mother rescues us as she comes up the stairs, looking harried again. "Helen and Nat and Grandma and Grandpa are here."

Too early. Now Grandma will have time to go poking into the kitchen. My father finishes his shoes and almost runs into their room to get dressed.

Still avoiding my room, I go into my parents' bedroom and talk to my mother while she dresses. From the window I see Phil arrive with his parents. His intelligent face is sunburned and he is very handsome and I'm going to marry him in about an hour, but I have not the slightest idea what he is thinking. The eeriness of it sends a sudden tightness to my throat, and I stay at the window so Mom can't see. A little later Phil's sister Gail arrives with her husband. She is expecting her first child in a few days; her feet are so swollen she is wearing loafers cut open at the heel. We are cruel to make her come out, even for a wedding — especially for a wedding.

I zip my mother into a navy blue dress which is simple

and not at all new and watch her put on a little powder and lipstick. She has forgotten George for the moment, and her eyes glow with excitement for the first time all day. I kiss her quickly before she goes downstairs.

Finally I go to my room. In a corner my wedding dress stands propped by mounds of tissue paper; it is a delicate, headless, armless bride. The thermometer outside the window registers ninety-six. Once, when I was about seven, it read nine below zero. That was an important day!

So is this. Yet all I feel is out of sorts. If we can just get through this evening, by tomorrow we'll be settled in our apartment on the lake where we will spend the summer. Phil's smile in the photograph on my desk cheers me up. When Mother and Barbara come in I can see from their faces that I'm beginning to look like a bride.

"How's everything?" I ask.

"Fine," Barbara says, slightly surprised, which means that my grandparents are behaving. Just as I get into my dress we hear a scuffling. Here they are with Dad, who looks helpless. Before I have time to put on my shoes I am told to sit down, and my grandparents take out a white handkerchief knotted at the four corners. Then they walk around me murmuring a Hebrew prayer.

"It's supposed to be a purification rite," my father whispers. "The handkerchief represents the earth." But the explanation does not satisfy. I feel like witches' brew.

Then Grandpa disappears with Dad, but Grandma lingers to rub the stuff of my dress between her roughened fingers. She is shrunken now, but still pretty.

"Here, Ma." My mother hands her the veil and she places it on me and the photographer who appears from nowhere snaps a picture. Grandma sighs with pleasure. I wink at Mom, yet I'm a little hurt by my grandfather's cursory treatment of me. He is strange, but I like him.

Barbara senses how I feel.

"Grandpa had to make sure Phil signs the *ketubah*," she says. Of course, the marriage contract, written in Hebrew. "Phil says it might be a conscription into the Israeli army for all he knows." We laugh, the photographer clicks away. I'm still not sure why we had to have a photographer. I recall saying, jokingly, that all we need is an album.

Barbara stays with me while we wait for Phil's grandmother. She is coming from the Bronx by subway and train. Someone has gone to meet her. As Barbara watches a purple finch duck its head in the big oak outside our window, I look at her thin shoulders. How grown up she is. The dress she is wearing was bought a year ago for me, but it never looked right; and now, seeing it look so well on her makes me feel old. Finished, somehow.

"Here they are," she says. But we hear only silence.

"Nana wasn't on the train," someone calls. A worried whispering emanates through the house. My mother decides to serve the hors d'oeuvres and drinks; the rabbi goes back to mourn with Sylvia Bernstein; one by one they ascend the stairs to visit me, exiled by tradition in my room.

Aunt Helen, a round bundle of a woman, takes my face in her hands and kisses me. She helps me take my dress off, gently, as if I were hurt. Then Mother enters. She and Helen look at each other, incredulous. In our family we don't let widowed, seventy-two-year-old grandmothers come from the Bronx to Long Island alone. This is now their family, they are thinking.

"She's very independent," I say. But they don't even bother to answer. And disappear.

Soon Dad arrives behind the largest fan in the house; the bride must be cool.

I lie down and the fan creates a breeze about my legs. Way down the block, near the big curve, some kids are playing baseball; near the chimney crickets ricochet in the grass; looking like Miss Muffets, the hollyhock along the side of the house push invisibly upward; plates clatter in the kitchen; Uncle Nat walks heavily down the hall. He feels guilty about being at my wedding while the rest of my aunts and uncles are cursing my parents at home. I pretend to doze and he goes away.

The next one is Max. I open one eye. We laugh.

"You look drunk that way," he says as I sit up in my slip, not at all embarrassed. He diapered me.

Suddenly I'm angry that they are all laughing and eating and drinking and I'm up here. "Isn't this ridiculous?"

"Yes," he says. "By the way, there was a wildcat subway strike at rush hour. We finally put on the radio."

The phone rings. It is almost nine. Max leaves. Barbara comes down the hall.

"Nana's at the station. Phil has gone to get her. Mom is calling the rabbi." She smoothes my hair. I get into the dress for the second time. On goes the veil.

From the hall I see pastel movement through the dark wood banisters. Then I am alone. The music starts. The wrong band. Inevitably. It begins again on the right spot. I walk down the stairs, Barbara walks ahead, Erica smiles, my mother holds out her arms as if to catch me, my father takes my arm. One of us, maybe both, is trembling, so I walk very close to him.

We stop. The rabbi smiles. I relax and smile back. But Grandpa's sharp blue eyes are severe. The rabbi assumes his pulpit manner, then begins. I don't hear a word. Phil steps forward and stands beside me. Now Grandpa is speaking in Yiddish, the fastest Yiddish spoken on this earth, then Phil places the ring on my fourth finger. Grandma jumps forward with a small cry and replaces it on my index finger. This is because the Talmud says it is more visible there, easier for the witnesses at a wedding to see. I can feel my mother stiffen behind me, but no one else cares where the ring is. Then there is the taste of the wine — too sweet — and the crunch of the broken glass, and Erica playing the wedding march on the piano while Phil kisses me, too tired of waiting to be shy about it.

The veil is whisked off me. Everyone kisses everyone else. My grandfather presses a pen into my hand and I sign the marriage contract. He looks at me, pleased, as if surprised I know how to write my own name. I place the ring back on my fourth finger, my grandmother frowns, someone slaps a bunch of telegrams into my hand. I greet Phil's grandma. She presses my arm and tears fill her eyes. "Am I glad to be alive!" she says.

Through dinner Phil and I scarcely talk. Despite all his careful plans it has been a long evening. In his eyes I see "Let's get out of here." I know it well; I have seen it for four years across lecture rooms, at parties, in stations, quadrangles, streets. But we can't move. Besides, we have years together. I see our life stretched out before me as clearly as the table, its settings, the food, the glasses. There will be lots of time.

"We must be patient," I whisper. He nods, but his eyes are still saying, "Let's get out of here."

It is getting cooler, the others are very gay. The photographer makes silly jokes so we smile, plates are rushed in laden and are taken away quietly, empty. Only Grandma won't eat. She nibbles some bread and drinks the champagne, but that's all. Mother has given up, I see, as she watches the old lady. Not even the ,dessert, the fabulous, chemically made ice cream will Grandma touch. I am filled with unreasonable hatred for her old, shriveled ways.

The cake is brought in, but I don't force myself to eat it; it can be frozen. "We can eat wedding cake all summer," I whisper to Phil, and this elicits the first real laugh from him all evening.

Spoons tinkle on glasses. My grandfather rises, holding an envelope. It is almost midnight, but he goes on and on. He is talking about the responsibilities of marriage, my father translates as he stands hunched behind us. Dad is proud of his vigorous father, and the old man's tactlessness doesn't surprise him. He has known his father for over fifty years.

Grandpa is finished. Finally. We get up from the table slowly, too full. Yet once up I revive. Just as I am beginning to enjoy myself Barbara draws me aside. It is time for us to leave. For the third time that evening she and Erica watch over me as I change and comb my hair and put on lipstick, and for the first time since we have known each other there is nothing to say. They kiss me very hard, then Mother comes upstairs. She isn't happy. Somewhere the wedding fell short of her ideal. But she is careful to let me know that I had nothing to do with it.

"You were beautiful, darling," she says, straightening my collar. I go into the kitchen to thank the caterer (why, I don't know, but we have been brought up to do such things) and kiss Jean, who has had a good cry. As I pass through the breakfast room I look up. The light shines through the spider's web; it is intact though the spider is gone. Then into the study, where Phil is getting the suitcases.

My father comes in. He looks confused. Put upon, almost, which is odd for him.

"Where is she going?" he asks my mother in a strange, harsh voice. She looks at him quizzically, and now I know why she has been so nervous all day. She starts to say something, but finally I am too impatient to wait for her explanation. I throw my arms around my parents and they kiss me, making a sandwich of me as they used to when I was little. Then we move apart, and as I take Phil's hand I see that his eyes are clear and filled with light.

Children
in the Park

EACH MORNING, JESSICA AND I WALKED FROM CAMP-
den Hill Road along Notting Hill Gate to the Kensington
Gardens playground. We had come to London three
weeks ago, at the beginning of June, and we were to stay
for a year. Phil had a job with an English firm. Some days
Jess and I lingered in front of the jeweler's window or at
the bookstore. Sometimes we bought buns at the patisserie,
and we never passed the window of the German delicatessen without marveling at the great sausages hanging there.
Once we had passed MacFisheries, Jess became impatient.
When she saw the gate to the playground, she started to
run.

As I watched her, I wondered if anyone would talk to us
that day. So far, no one had said a word. Jess didn't seem to
mind. She was just four and happy to be pushed on the
swings or go down the slide or pretend she was taking a
trip in the huge rocking boat. After she got to know the
playground, I would take out my knitting or a book, and
as long as she could run over to me or blow a kiss she was
content.

Still, it was lonely. And as I sat and watched the English
children and their mothers I began to be uncomfortable.

The children were so blond and talkative, the mothers so dark and taciturn. When I described this to our only English friend, a bachelor who worked with Phil, he howled. "Those aren't the mothers," he said. "They're the au pair girls."

From then on, I looked for the few children who were brought to the park by their mothers. I sat as close as I decently could to these women, but they were involved with their children or each other and there never seemed to be a chance to break in and introduce myself. I had always been shy, and as the days passed it was harder and harder to smile.

Finally, on a strangely quiet Fourth of July, Jess found a friend, a little Indian boy named Raja. The children played, and Raja's mother and I sat together. They were in London for a week while Raja's father attended a conference. She was sweet and gentle and had read a good many American books. Raja was her first child. We were soon comfortable with each other.

The breezes that week were soft. Southern England hadn't had such a good summer in years; the papers and radio were astonished by it. We went to Round Pond almost every day to feed the ducks; twice we picnicked — first on American food, then on Indian. The roses seemed to multiply before our eyes, and on our last day we went to Hampton Court and took photographs of the children sniffing the flowers; then we kissed good-bye.

The next day Jess announced, "I'm not going to the park today. I shall miss Raja too much." In the time we had been here, she had begun to sound like an American's idea of an English child.

I smiled.

"Don't laugh at me, Mommy," she said and started to cry. She was usually such a cheerful child that it upset me. I suggested that for a treat we go the long way, past Princess Margaret's house and through the Orangery, which meant that we would enter the playground at the back.

Right next to the back gate was a child who seemed to be waiting for us. I had noticed him the day before at the statue of Peter Pan. He had watched Jessica point out to Raja all the tiny animals hidden in the statue. When he saw me watching him now he looked frightened, so I lowered my eyes. When I looked up he was gone. Then he was back again. He held open the gate. I said, "Thank you." He didn't answer and darted ahead of us. When Jess went off to the rocking boat he followed her, staying always a few feet behind.

He was the thinnest child I had ever seen — so flat and angular he looked like a paper doll. In his short faded pants his legs were all bone and knobby knees; his wrists and ankles were no bigger than Jessica's, though he was several years older.

His face was one of those beautiful homely faces that children have when one feature seems to have grown a little ahead of the others: small nose, much-too-wide mouth, biggish ears, a nice firm chin, and small, almost black, eyes. His brown hair was dull and very thin — it reminded me of newborn hair — and though it was cut in a neat bang across his forehead it flopped as he ran through the playground, never taking his eyes off Jess.

Jess always left the swings for last, and before we did them we usually had a snack. The child lingered near us. I offered him a cracker; he hesitated but finally shook his head and ran away.

"Who is he?" Jess asked.

"I don't know."

"Maybe he's my friend. He looks like a marionette."

As we left by the front gate we looked for him. I thought I saw him behind the little brick house where the matron was stationed, but he didn't come out, so perhaps I had been wrong.

That night Jess told her father about her friend, and the next morning it was clear that she expected to see him again.

"He may not be there today. He may have to go somewhere," I warned her on the way to the park.

"He'll be there. I know he will. I feel it in my bones," she said to make me laugh.

He was waiting for us at the front gate. He must have watched us leave by the front the day before. He seemed less frightened. When Jess said, "Good morning," he smiled. He swung on the gate as we went through. We waited for him; after a few seconds he joined us.

"What's your name?" I asked.

His reply was so soft that I had to bend down to hear. "She's Jess, you're Mum, I'm Pat-rick."

Patrick stayed next to Jess that day. He shared our snack. When I pushed Jess on the swing, he stood far enough away not to get hurt and made funny faces to amuse her; she laughed and laughed. When we were getting ready to leave, he tapped me on the arm and pointed to a very high slide. At the bottom of its ladder was a sign: ONLY CHILDREN TEN YEARS OLD AND UP CAN GO ON THIS

SLIDE. Patrick climbed the ladder slowly, he waved to Jessica when he reached the top. Then, as if it were nothing at all, he slid down the slide. We clapped for him.

He walked us to the gate. "I was ten in March," he explained. When we looked back, he was swinging on the gate as if he had nothing else in the world to do.

Each day we found Patrick where we left him. The days got warmer and lazier, and we walked to Round Pond and fed the ducks. We began to bring lunch. At first I brought a sandwich for Patrick; after two days he produced his own brown bag. Before he ate, he showed me a thick cheese sandwich on whole wheat bread and an orange. "Mum knows I like oranges," he said shyly.

We knew nothing about his family except that there were a mother and father and several children. If Jess or I asked the names of his brothers and sisters, he would reel off a different list each time, like the ending of *Rumpelstiltskin*. When I asked Patrick where he lived, he pointed toward Bayswater Road but named no street.

The weather was still glorious. Sometimes we stayed in the park after lunch. If Jess was sleepy, she napped on a blanket while I read in the green canvas chair I got from the chair man for sixpence. Patrick would go off for a walk, but he always managed to return just as Jess was waking up. Then they would roll Jess's ball in and out among the plane trees or play marbles on a piece of flat grass. Patrick was a good player. I kept his marble collection for him each morning while he was in the playground. When he handed it to me, I had the feeling he was trusting me with his life.

Sometimes the two children sat under a tree and talked quietly. Patrick had made up a tale about a large family in the country. One day they were elves, another day they were people. The family was energetic — always building something — and happy. In the beginning Patrick did all the telling of his story, but after a while Jess made up some characters, and once I heard him say, "Now that's an interesting person, Jess." They were an appealing picture: the thin, earnest boy and the dark, curly-haired little girl intent on every word he said. People smiled as they passed them.

Although I was still quick to spot the regulars in the park, it didn't matter so much that they ignored us. Jessica had a friend and I had begun to relax. There was a pleasant rhythm to our days. Patrick was a natural mimic. He loved to imitate the lady whose boxer broke away from her to have a daily swim in Round Pond. Or the hysterical mother of a little boy named Andrew, who was forever lost. Or the old man who found us at lunchtime, ate his lunch beside us, then covered his face with the London *Times* and snored for two hours. When Patrick was miming someone, he seemed to disappear. The shy wariness that seemed so much a part of him was gone.

"You'll be an actor, Patrick. I know it," I told him once, and he blushed with pride.

The English school year runs well into July, and when I realized that Patrick was the oldest child in the park in the mornings, I asked him why he wasn't in school.

"I been sick, and I go back to school in the autumn," he said. "After the August holiday." That seemed to explain his thinness, so I accepted it.

One afternoon, Jess asked if we could all go to Mac-Fisheries for some candy. I noticed that Patrick walked slowly and reluctantly. We were tired. It had been a hot day.

In front of the candy assortment each child held my hand. It was the first time Patrick had taken my hand, and I was pleased.

Suddenly we heard a harsh voice. "Go on, get outa here. There's nothin' for you here!" I didn't pay attention until I felt a sharp tap on the shoulder. A large man in a dirty white apron was standing over us. "He yours?" he said, and then he shrugged. "Nah, he's not yours."

"He's our friend."

"He's a fruit thief, that's what he is." He bent as if to cuff Patrick on the ear, but the boy ducked and the man lumbered back to the fruit section.

I quickly paid for the candy that Patrick and Jess had chosen; we left the store hastily. When we got outside and had walked a way toward the park, I turned to Patrick. "Did you take his fruit?"

"No'm," he said. "One day I had some pennies and I was trying to figure if I could buy an orange, but I'm slow, you know, and he thought I took one." The child wasn't lying.

From then on it was understood that we stay in the park. Soon the playground and all of Kensington Gardens was crowded — school was out; it was holiday. I persisted in my game of smiling at all likely Englishwomen, and sometimes I got a smile back and a few times a sentence or two. One woman greeted me with "How's SuperAmerica?" and insisted on our exchanging names and addresses, but nothing came of it.

At the end of the holiday there was to be a puppet show in the playground. Fliers were handed out early in the week, and on the day of the show Patrick came dressed in his best clothes. He and Jess and I got seats in the front row. A woman and her boy sat down next to us. We had seen them occasionally. She smiled. "Big day," she said.

"I should say." I turned to the children. "Isn't it?"

"Are they both yours?"

"No, just Jessica. This is Patrick."

"And who is Patrick?"

"A friend of ours. We meet him in the park almost every day."

"Where does he live?"

"I don't know," I said.

As if to help me, she leaned over and asked Patrick, "What school do you go to?"

He didn't answer.

"He hasn't been to school for a while," I said. "He's been sick."

"Is that what he told you? Cunning child. He doesn't look sick."

"He's very thin and if he says he's been sick, he's been sick, I'm sure of that."

She looked at me suspiciously. "My sister said Americans were strange. She went there last summer. So gullible, she said." She took her child's hand and moved away from us. Soon someone else sat down and the show began. It was an excellent production of *Cinderella*, and Patrick and Jess were thrilled. They clapped hard at the end.

As we were walking out I said rather too lightly, "Patrick, where *do* you live?" But the minute I asked the question I knew it was no use.

"In a flat, 'm," he answered with exaggerated politeness, and he and Jess went off into giggles. No one was going to tell me anything that day.

School started, and Patrick continued to meet us in the playground. When I asked him about it he said, "My school starts later." By this time I knew there was something wrong with Patrick that was not merely physical sickness. He reminded me of a pollarded tree that had been neglected and had begun to sprout branches in some directions but not in others. For one thing, he could read only the simplest words, and those stumblingly. Yet he could tell splendid stories — some based on the beginnings of fairy tales, some his own. He had trouble counting, yet he knew the name and habits of every bird that passed us in our wanderings through the park. When I admired his marble collection, he began to tell me about glass — how it was made and colored and the different grades.

"How do you know so much about glass?" I said.

"An old man I used to know worked at the glassworks up north. We liked to pass the time," he said. "He was my friend."

We went to Europe for three weeks in October, and when we returned Jess was sure Patrick wouldn't be in the park; we didn't hurry the first morning. But when we saw the gate, there he was. It looked as if he had been swinging on that gate ever since we left.

"School starts in a few weeks," he said to me before he grabbed Jess's hand.

The days grew shorter and cooler, but compared to Westchester it was a mild fall. Roses bloomed into the beginning of November; the trees still had their green leaves. Because the weather was good, Jess and I decided to take Patrick to the Regent's Park Zoo. We planned to be gone most of the day, and I felt it was necessary to get permission from Patrick's parents. I explained this to him, expecting him to give me a telephone number. Instead, he said, "Could you write a note for me, Mum? We don't have a telephone."

He brought me a note in an illegible scrawl. With effort I deciphered: "Patrick can go. Thank you. Ivy W————." The surname was a wiggly line. But the note was obviously authentic, and when the day came Patrick was waiting for us at the park in his best clothes, with his lunch and a bag of sweets for Jess.

The chimpanzees' tea party was the highlight of the day. After we had gone back to see the chimps three more times, I insisted that we start for home. The sky was streaked orange and gold; the air was chilly.

We got out of the bus at Kensington Gardens to drop Patrick off. I had no intention of going into the playground and was looking forward to a cup of hot coffee and a different pair of shoes when Jess pulled at my arm. "Mommy, look at those funny people."

In the playground was a gang of young boys dressed up in tattered clothes. "It's Guy Fawkes Day," Patrick said.

Jess insisted on going closer.

"A penny for the Guy! A penny for the Guy!" the boys called when we approached them. I opened my handbag to get some pennies, and Patrick and Jess slipped away to the swings. I could feel dusk coming. I wanted to leave. Patrick's parents would worry; it was past teatime.

Suddenly a voice called, "There's Patrick!" and the boys left me and ran toward the swings.

"Where ya been, Patrick?" one called.

Patrick didn't answer and began to swing higher.

"We miss ya at school!" another yelled.

I ran over to Jessica's swing and stopped it. "Come on, Patrick. It's time to go home," I said loudly.

He stared as if he didn't know me and pumped harder.

The boys were chanting: "We'll catch Patrick and kick Patrick and hit him with stones, and after he's dead we'll just stamp on his bones."

"Get out of here!" I shouted, but they laughed and chanted the same words again. Patrick swung higher and higher, and I had a horrible vision of him going as high as he could and then falling to the ground in a pool of blood.

"Get out of here! Get out of here!" I yelled, but the boys didn't listen and it was useless to call for help because the playground was empty; the matron had gone home.

I turned my back on the boys and began to talk to Patrick. When he swung toward me I could see that his eyes were glazed.

"Patrick!" I called his name several times. He stared but didn't answer.

Jess tugged my hand. "Patrick!" she screamed. "Patrick, it's Jess!"

He looked down.

"Come on, Patrick. It's time to go," I called.

With that he stopped pumping and let the swing slow down. The playground felt unnaturally quiet; for a moment I thought the boys might be hiding, ready to pounce on him. But then I saw them walking toward Bayswater Road, calling, "A penny for the Guy! A penny for the Guy!" I held the two children close and we waited until we couldn't hear them anymore, then we hurried out of the park.

"They were from my last school," Patrick said, and I squeezed his hand. We watched him turn off Bayswater Road and we waved good-bye; Jessica and I caught the bus home.

The next day Patrick wasn't in the park, or the next, or the next. At first, I tried to make our search for him a game of hide-and-seek, but neither Jess nor I felt like playing at it. We became more concerned; finally one morning I approached the matron at the playground. She was standing at the door of the little brick house, her thin coat pulled tightly around her, for suddenly the weather had become cold and damp. She was not quick to smile, but she was not unkind with the children. In the summer, when Jess had scraped her knee, she had helped us wash and bandage it. A few days after that she seemed about to say something to me — I think about Patrick, because she had pointed to him. Then she had thought better of it and said, abruptly, "Never mind."

"Do you know where Patrick could be?" I asked her. Jess had consented to go on the swings for a few minutes.

"Hasn't shown up, has he?" she asked.

"No, not for a few days." Actually, it was exactly three days. "And he never said good-bye. I'd like to get in touch with him."

She shrugged. "I don't know how. I don't know where he lives and I don't know his people's name." She paused. "There's something wrong with him, you know. His mum came here once and said if he got too wild I was to take him by the shoulders and tell him to go home. Loud. But he never got wild, just jumped around a lot. Until you came. With you and the little girl he seemed happy. Though I never understood why you were interested in the likes o' him." She had planted her hands on her hips and was shaking her head. She looked at me thoughtfully.

"Did his mother say what was wrong?"

"She didn't seem to know. Poor people they are, lots of children. Said they had told them he was disturbed or retarded — one or the other. Couldn't seem to make up their minds. You know, psychologists and the like."

"Did she say anything about school?"

"She did say he'd be going off to a boarding home in Scotland one of these days — they thought they could help him if he lived away. Make him more manageable. I guess he's gone." She looked at me for a moment and her voice softened. "Don't worry. He'll make his way," she said. "They always do. They have to."

Rescue

SUNSHINE WASHED THE AZALEAS AND HOLLY BUSHES with such a glistening light that the leaves looked as if they had been dipped in oil. The rocks in the wall he and Gloria had built when the kids were little suddenly held a kaleidoscope of colors he had never noticed before.

He walked the dog up the street, then around the block. Caleb was already out.

"Hello, son. I've got to get the begonias into the greenhouse," Caleb told him. "Frost tonight."

"I heard." Allie smiled.

Every morning he and Caleb talked a little while the rest of the neighborhood was still sleeping behind drawn drapes and shades. But today the beauty of the morning seemed to mock him. Up early, out walking the dog at six-thirty. For what?

Quietly he opened the kitchen door and started to make coffee. Gloria loved the smell of it as she woke up. Then he set out some food for the dog, scrambled himself two eggs, and put the toast down. Allie was about to sit down when Gloria came in. "What a gorgeous day!" she greeted him. He could see that her eyes were troubled, he knew that she was trying with as much will as she could to forget for one day, for a space of time between a glorious sunup and what would probably be a spectacular sunset that Allie, her childhood sweetheart, her friend, her lover, her husband, the father of her three children, was out of work for the first time in his life.

Allie knew she had never worried about him, till now. When they were still in high school only she had known how different he was. Everyone else thought he would become a teacher; even now he was often mistaken for a teacher with his glasses, his thick graying hair, his rough tweeds that hung loosely on his lean body, the pipe that was stuck between his teeth or poked out of his pocket. But Allie couldn't have lived cooped up indoors all day. He had always been good with his hands, so after he graduated from college he had learned the mason's trade. Building appealed to his mind and heart, he brought home a good living, and Gloria knew he was happy. Only his parents were uncomfortable about his work. When people asked what he did they said quickly, "Alexander's in construction." His name disappointed them, too. They had chosen a name with dignity, with the weight of history upon it. And what had it become? Allie! It sounded like a girl's name, yet it was the name that everyone — his wife, his friends, his children — called him.

"Hi, Allie." Nora, his eldest, kissed him on the nose. She was all smiles, he knew she wanted a favor.

"Allie, could you run my bike up to the shop? They said they could put the rack on this week. I have enough money now, it's on my desk, and they'll put it on while you wait."

"Say, Allie, there's a shelf in my closet that's hanging by

a thread. Could you screw it into the wall? It probably needs a molly." Allie stared at his son. But Roger was absolutely serious. Lately Allie had the feeling that the two older children were finding all kinds of chores for him just to keep him busy. It annoyed and touched him at the same time.

Only the little one, only Katie, their six-year-old, greeted him without a request. She was a slow riser, still warm with sleep. She climbed into his lap.

"Now this is a pleasure no workingman has," Allie said softly into her tangled hair, but from the quick frowns and worried looks he knew he had said the wrong thing.

They ate in silence. To divert them Allie gestured toward the patterns of sunlight on the kitchen counter. "Look at the squiggly lines!" he said. He startled Katie; she jumped, and Allie's coffee spilled.

"Oh, Allie!" Gloria was exasperated.

"Sorry," he said and drank the new cup of coffee she put before him too soon. He scalded his throat.

It was the sixteenth day he was out of work, the beginning of the fourth week, no relief in sight. Between the union benefits and unemployment they were all right, but that didn't fill the time from eight to four. He had thought it would be a good chance to catch up on all the chores. Now he'd better get going. He knew where his list was, he had been using it as a bookmark. Allie went up the stairs, two at a time, whistling.

Clean gutters
Fix porch screen

Drain hot water heater
Look at sleeping bags — take to cleaner if needed
Dig beds for bulbs
Plane kids' bathroom door
Paint porch chairs

His heart sank, but what had he expected? There were good reasons why jobs found themselves on lists. It was a good day for the gutters and the digging. He could also paint — the chairs would dry fast today, but they needed oil paint and the brushes had to be cleaned with turpentine and he knew Gloria would be annoyed, again, if he brought them into the kitchen late in the afternoon. Once more she would say, "If only we had put a sink in the cellar." She had wanted to, years ago, and now it was impossible. The price, even if he had been working, was ridiculous.

After he dug the holes under the ash tree Gloria helped him carry out the bulbs. He could see that she expected him to help her, although she usually did the planting herself. He could hear Tom Martinson and his wife behind the hedge. They worked in their garden every morning. That was all right for old men like Tom or Caleb, but not for him, not today, anyway.

"I'll start on the gutters. I think they're full," he muttered.

She started to sort the bulbs. She had bought them weeks ago; it was getting late to plant the little ones. Now he wondered if she would have bought bulbs at all after he lost his job.

So he stood there, because the thought depressed him,

and watched her. He had always loved her long hands and skinny wrists, and now, seeing them mix bone meal into the earth and smooth it all and set the bulbs in place, their little points looking like so many elves' caps, Allie was filled with desire for his wife. What he really wanted was to suggest they go inside and turn down the bed and make love in broad daylight, as they did when they got away by themselves, or long ago when Nora was a baby. But now there seemed something obscene about it — he hanging around out of work, and besides, Hazel Parker was taking her morning constitutional, and the Martinsons were talking softly on the other side of the hedge, and when he squinted he could see little Danny Wexler riding his kiddy car on the patio while his mother hung up her morning's wash. So he mumbled to Gloria's questioning look, "I'm going for the ladder."

Instead of the usual foul-smelling mess, the leaves in the gutters were dry, crumbly, and had a faint sour-sweet smell. He didn't even need gloves. Quickly he scooped up the leaves and dumped them into the heavy plastic bag he had hung on the ladder. Every few minutes he had to climb down and move the ladder; the gutters weren't as dirty as he thought. Then he remembered he had paid Roger and a friend to clean them last spring. Oh, well, he was here, he would do the rest.

Suddenly his hand touched something. Weightless in his hand, the bird felt like another pulse as Allie carried it down the ladder. It was a goldfinch — the female — yellowish olive feathers and that fat little finch bill.

"Look," he said. But Gloria didn't hear; she was back on her heels, her head cocked to one side making a decision.

He stepped closer. "Look." He practically thrust the bird into her face when she turned.

"Oh, Allie." Vertical lines appeared between her eyes. "What should we do?" she asked. It was what he wanted to hear, although they both knew that the kindest thing would be to put the bird in the woods to die. "Maybe it's a broken wing." Gloria touched the finch's feathers with the pad of her index finger.

Allie had the feeling it was more than a broken wing; something about the bird's stare unsettled him, and as he was about to say something about putting it in the woods, the throbbing in his hand stopped.

He wanted to close the bird's eyes. He was on the volunteer ambulance corps, and after he had watched a few people die, he understood that old custom of putting coins on a dead man's eyes, or at least closing the lids. In the cellar he found an old shoe box and smoothed the tissue paper left in it and laid the bird in it. Then he put a rubber band around the box and put it into the garbage can. He finished the gutters before lunch.

All the climbing up and down had not been good for his left knee. It was a tender spot — too much basketball in high school and college. Gloria saw him grimace as he sat down to lunch.

"Your knee?"

He nodded.

"Why don't you lie down after lunch and read? On the porch." She smiled. "You haven't done that in a long time."

"The chairs need painting."

"They'll wait."

When he went upstairs to get his book she was at her desk paying bills. She had always done that; now she was putting them into piles the way she used to when they had first bought the house and there wasn't enough money to pay them all at once.

"Glory, I wish I could tell you how rotten . . ." The sentence dwindled as he put his hands on her shoulders.

"Never mind." She shrugged his hands away. Her voice was curt and dry, as it always was when she felt pressed about money. "We'll manage," she said coldly. "I'll get a job" was implicit in the words; Allie knew they would have to talk about that soon if things didn't improve.

He picked up *Fire in the Lake* and started out of the room.

"Why are you reading something so depressing?"

"I'll read what I like," he said brusquely.

The porch was like another world. The furniture had belonged to Gloria's parents; they had painted and re-covered it, but when Allie was out here he always felt he had walked back into the years when he and Gloria were still courting. The children sometimes complained that the porch looked so old-fashioned, couldn't they get new plastic stuff that didn't need painting, but he and Gloria always refused. Allie lay down on the couch and pushed a pillow behind his head.

He must have been reading for about an hour when the alarm sounded. Four — the ambulance call. Allie jumped up, grabbed his jacket from the closet, and was taking his wallet and keys from the mail basket when Gloria called from the top of the stairs, "Allie, your knee! You're not even on duty." Her voice was high because she knew he would ignore her. She had never understood his devotion to the ambulance corps, but what he heard now was different — a mixture of shame and concern for him. Not many people knew he was out of work, but what did that matter? He had to go. He heard himself say, "You're crazy, Gloria," as he closed the door and ran to the car.

He was the first at the ambulance building. The cop waiting said, "A heart attack, in the drugstore."

Allie ran down the small street that led to the shopping part of town. People milled around the entrance to the drugstore. Inside a cop had put an oxygen mask over the man's face. The man wasn't breathing.

"Get that off him. It doesn't help when they're not breathing," Allie said roughly to the cop, who frowned but did as he was told. Someone started breathing into the man's mouth. He looked up. "Name's Joe, I'm a fireman," he told Allie.

"How many minutes?" Allie asked.

"Just four, now," the druggist answered. Allie nodded. He still had time. For adults it was six minutes, for kids twelve, before brain damage started. He felt for a pulse. None. Allie kneeled next to the man; something cracked in his knee but he couldn't feel any pain. Now all he knew was that he had to get that heart going again. Press, then, "One, two, three, four, five." At five Joe breathed into the man's mouth. Press, count, press, count. In a few seconds Allie could feel the heart muscle begin to work. Press, count, press, count.

"They've got him going again," the druggist said to the few people who had lingered as he herded them out.

"Is that heart massage?" Allie heard a woman ask. Then a clatter of bottles falling and the store was empty. He and Joe and the man were alone until the ambulance crew came. He hoped it would be a good group. The man wasn't old; his face looked familiar, but Allie couldn't place it. He had had a bad heart attack.

"Okay, Allie?" A cop stood over him. He nodded. If he spoke he would break the rhythm and lose the whole thing. He once had had to do this for almost an hour, the ambulance had broken down. Press, count, press, count.

The door opened. He breathed easier. It was the best crew. Quickly they put the positive pressure oxygen mask on the man's face. Joe sat back against a display case rubbing his neck. Then someone said, "Jesus, it's Jack Werten, he's only fifty-two."

"Take it easy, Allie." He stopped for fifteen seconds while they put a board under Werten's back. A little while later he stopped again and they put Werten and the board on a stretcher. Press, count, press, count. They stopped one last time and moved Werten into the ambulance. Now one of the crew took over. Allie stood up. His first step was a limp, but he was only dimly aware of the pain in his knee.

"It looks like a bad one," Joe said. Allie nodded. He remembered that Werten's boy and Roger had been in cub scouts together. Werten was a funny, good-natured man, always willing to help out. Allie had a hunch he would make it. He was the kind who would fight back.

"Let me know how it goes," Allie said as they closed the doors. Then the whistle and they were gone.

Allie couldn't go home. He needed to get into a hot bath but he didn't want to see Gloria, hear her nag about his knee, watch his pain as he walked. He realized that for three weeks he had been hiding at home; when he had had an errand he had waited till after four, when he would have been home anyway, before he showed his face in the village. Now it was two-thirty. He went back to his car and checked his wallet. Fourteen bucks. Not a very princely sum, he smiled to himself. He should call Gloria, maybe pick up some groceries for her. But he didn't want to. He felt like he had the three times his kids were born, when the nurses had shooed him out of the hospital. "It's going to be a while," they had said each time. He should have stayed with Gloria to the end. They let fathers into the delivery room now, but he had been too dumb to insist. He regretted not seeing any of his children born.

What to do? He couldn't sit here all afternoon. He drove down to the main village parking lot and got out.

"That was great, Allie!" It was Teddy, the druggist, out for a smoke. He offered Allie a cigarette. Allie hadn't had one since college, but this felt good.

"I hope he makes it," Teddy said. "So young."

"I think he will."

Then Teddy's raised eyebrows. "Out of work?"

Allie nodded.

"Tough break." But Teddy was too busy to linger.

Allie walked past the post office into Big Top. He got the *Times*. Past the shoe store. Tracy, the owner, waved. He stopped to look at the kids' shoes.

"Looking for something, Allie?"

"I think so. Gloria said just the other day that Katie needed new shoes. What've you got?"

"Why don't you bring her in after school?" Tracy said.

"No, listen, let me get her some, for a surprise, then if they're not right Gloria can change them."

Tracy shrugged. "Taking the day off?"

"No, out of work. The fourth week."

Tracy brought down school shoes.

"Not, not those. The cute ones, the dressy kind, Mary Janes. That's what she needs," Allie reassured him and picked out black patent shoes with a T-strap.

"They're twelve ninety-five," Tracy warned.

"Here's ten bucks, the rest on account." Allie grinned. Tracy smiled back.

With the shoe box under his arm Allie knew what to do. He drove to the nursery. He and Gloria had spent days here when they were landscaping the house; he knew its layout like the back of his hand.

"Hey, Allie." It was a friend of Nora's who worked here part-time.

"Hi, Tim."

"Help you?"

"I'm looking for a piggyback, my wife's died over the summer. I think they're in the far greenhouse," Allie said.

"Right."

Allie liked nurseries, he had often thought that if he hadn't gone into the building trades he might have done something in landscaping. The mist hung heavily in the greenhouse, but it wasn't oppressive. And the plants looked so good! Allie picked out a full piggyback that was beginning to fall into an interesting asymmetrical shape. It would look fine hanging in the hall. The planter there had been empty all fall.

The plant was seven dollars. He charged it.

Then he drove to Korvette's and went to the record department. Here he would use his BankAmericard. He picked out an Elton John record for Nora and a Bob Dylan for Roger.

"Could you wrap those please? Gift wrap?" He asked the girl.

"There's an extra charge. Twenty-five cents each."

"Okay." Allie fished fifty cents from his pocket.

On his way home he stopped at the liquor store.

"Hello, Allie. Soave Bolla?" Allie nodded and looked in his wallet; he had only three dollars in bills and about thirty-five cents in change.

"Gee, I don't have enough," he said.

"Don't worry about it, you can make up the difference next time." Then the man added, "Gift wrap?"

"Sure, it's for my wife."

The minute Allie walked into the house he could feel Gloria's anger. It hung in the hall like the humidity in the greenhouse. He hated it.

"Hi, Allie." Nora came out of the living room. Suddenly Allie remembered her bike.

"Hi, kid. Listen, I didn't get to your bike, but we can run up now, if you want."

She shook her head. "Too much homework."

"I'll do it tomorrow, promise." He put the packages down on the hall table but she didn't seem curious and went off.

"Allie, Mom's been looking for you." Roger came up out of the cellar with some clothes. "She's folding clothes and mad. She said you went for an ambulance call at two and she needed the car."

Allie didn't say anything. He could hear Katie playing with a friend upstairs.

As she came into the hall Gloria's face over a pile of clothes was stony and distant.

"You might have called. I was planning to use the car."

"Sorry. I had some errands to do and I didn't think. I'm sorry."

She didn't answer and went upstairs.

"Did anyone call?" he asked Roger.

"Not while I've been here."

Allie opened the mail. He felt a little strange with all those packages next to him; quickly he put them into the hall closet. He could hear Gloria go into the kitchen. He knew the minute she lifted the lid of the stew pot.

"Say, that smells good," he said as he stood at the door to the kitchen. She didn't answer.

"Anyone call?" She shook her head.

He tried to put his arm around her waist as she opened the refrigerator. She stiffened.

"Oh, come on, Glory, I'm sure you didn't need the car that badly."

"It isn't the car. You seem to forget what you screamed when you left here in such a rush."

"Oh, that, I didn't mean that, you know I didn't. A man was sick, really sick. I had to go. You knew that."

"Yes, unfortunately. And now you're limping. You'd better go take a hot bath. There's time before dinner."

"No, I don't feel like it now."

"Suit yourself."

"Listen, Gloria, it was Jack Werten. His kid was in cub scouts with Roger. A heart attack."

Finally she reacted. "Oh, Allie, he's so young." Allie shrugged. He had thought that if she expressed interest in the ambulance call he would want to sit down and tell her about it, but suddenly he was tired. Maybe he'd better go up and take that bath. He left without saying a word.

When he was getting out of the tub the phone rang. It was Eve, from the ambulance corps. "They think he's going to make it, Allie. It was close, but the doctors think he has a good chance." Her voice was weary, yet content. Allie knew how spent she felt.

"Thanks, Eve, thanks a lot."

"Is he going to be okay?" Gloria asked as he came into the kitchen.

"They hope so. That was Eve. The doctors think he has a chance." Gloria smiled at him. A real smile. The first all day. "Come on, kids," she called. "Dinner."

"But before we sit down, I have a surprise. A lot of surprises," Allie said. He went to the hall closet and pulled out the packages and brought them into the dining room.

Gloria stared at him, bewildered. Then she exploded, "Presents! You were out getting presents when there's so much to do around here, when there isn't enough money to pay the bills! I'm sitting at my desk trying to figure out what to pay for and what bills I can hold and you're buying presents!" Her eyes flashed at him, she didn't even seem to see the kids. They held their presents a little away from their bodies, not quite sure what to do. But Allie simply looked at them and said, "Open your presents, kids." Gloria sank into her chair and put her head on her palms.

"Look, Mommy, new Mary Janes," Katie said. "Imagine

buying shoes for someone without them and having them fit! Only Allie could do that." The child was so pleased that Gloria forced herself to smile a narrow smile.

"Mommy, aren't you going to open yours?" Katie said. Gloria barely nodded. Nora and Roger liked their records, Allie could see. Now he pushed her presents toward Gloria.

"These are for you," he said quietly.

She opened them slowly. He could see that she liked the plant. Her voice was grudging, though. "This can go into the planter in the hall." Then, "Nice wine." She looked directly at Allie. She was waiting for an explanation. A hardness had settled in her eyes.

He just shrugged.

"I wish you would tell me what the big occasion is," she said. No one answered. "Why we needed presents today," she added.

"Because we did," Allie said firmly. "We just did."

The Running

"WHERE SHALL WE EAT?" HE LOOKED UP FROM THE paper. There were dark circles under his eyes. She stared at him.

"Eat," he said. "You have to eat. You have three small children to take care of when you get home. And you will have piles of laundry and there will be dust under the beds. You've been away for ten days."

"You forget" — she smiled — "that Paolo is a much better housekeeper than me."

"Um-m, that's true." He took another sip of his drink, his fourth. She wanted to say something about that, but he anticipated her.

"Don't worry — I won't get drunk. You forget how much I used to drink in the old days."

It was true. When she was growing up, an only cherished child, she used to think everyone's father sat down at five in the afternoon and drank six or seven Scotches. It wasn't at all strange to her then, for he did it, as he did everything, with such grace. And he never drank at any other time. His drinking hadn't seemed to worry her mother — odd, now that she thought about it. If Paolo

drank that much, she would wonder what was wrong with
their life. But her mother used to sit there quietly, sewing
or crocheting, smoking much too much and listening.

It was best on clear winter dusks. Whenever she was
away from home she would picture them then. As the long
cavern of Park Avenue fell into shadow her mother would
turn on a few lamps but leave the curtains open, so that
they could watch the sky purple and finally blacken. Her
vibrant, red-haired mother sitting in her favorite, green
velvet chair — the same chair she herself sat in now, its
green velvet hidden by the flowered chintz slipcover. Who
had put the summer slipcovers on? She stroked the fabric
and looked at him. He was staring at her just as he used to
when she was in her teens and waiting for her date to
arrive.

"Your mother reminded me to ask the maid to put them
on."

"You're uncanny." She threw up her hands in hyper-
bolic resignation.

"Paolo will be the same with your girls. Fathers can read
daughters' minds." When he said it, it became a fact. She
wanted to kiss him; since her marriage ten years ago their
kisses had dwindled to hello and good-bye, and sometimes,
in the tumult of the children, not even that. A kiss now
would startle him. Besides, he was back to his paper. Something caught his eye; from habit he took out a fat red
pencil and marked it to be cut out later. He looked up.

"You still haven't said where you want to eat, and it's
Friday night and we should make a reservation."

"Let's wait," she said. "I'm not that hungry and I'm sure
you don't need a reservation on a Friday night in August.
Everyone has taken off for the weekend." The truth was,

he never needed a reservation, but it was part of his code to pretend he was like everyone else.

"Okay, but don't tell me later you want just a sandwich. You've eaten enough sandwiches this summer to last a decade."

She was taking a sleeper back to her family upstate. It seemed as if she had been commuting to New York for years, but actually it was twelve weeks. For a moment she allowed herself the luxury of thinking of her children, of their big, cheerful house, old and cluttered even after she had cleaned. So different from this gracious apartment, with its polished rosewood and cherry tables and pale rugs and printed slipcovers and draperies.

Huge clumps of blue and white asters were scattered in vases exactly as her mother liked them. "Must stop for some flowers," he had murmured as they went out through the heavy doors of the hospital. She knew better than to question him when he was so determined. She didn't even protest when they went to a strange florist. No questions and no answers about anything but the flowers themselves. Because he made it seem so natural, she let her arms be filled with the beautiful asters. In the taxi, and back in the apartment as they filled the old crystal vases, she let herself be drawn into the illusion he seemed bent on creating, so that now, standing there touching the flowers, she wondered if it was true that her mother had died as the early morning fog began to burn off the East River.

"Of course she did," she said out loud. Her father didn't hear her because by then she was on her way to the guest room, controlling a compulsion to touch everything she passed.

"It's really the children's room," her mother used to say to the occasional overnight guest. "Alexandra's children's room when they come to New York." It was wallpapered in wide orange and yellow stripes and there were bunk beds, a crib, baskets of toys and all her old books.

She saw her mother sitting on the floor, playing cassino with the girls, her mother's elegant clothes tucked under her legs, her remarkably vivid red hair straying over her forehead as she let her granddaughters discover the fine points of the game. If there was a family game, it was cassino, and her mother played it with her children as her parents had played it with her on those wonderfully peaceful winter dusks.

Winter dusks. How the mind travels in circles. She remembered how she would rush with her French so she could go into the living room and sit with her parents.

"Finished your French, pet?" her mother would say, and she would nod happily. She would read or knit, and when the smells from the kitchen where Bessie was humming were almost too pungent to bear, her mother would pull out the cards and they would play cassino. Sometimes it was just the two of them and sometimes her father would join in.

"It's such a middle-brow game," her mother once said. "We should have learned bridge."

"Then," her father replied with a smile around his eyes, "we would have needed a second child."

"Um-m, I suppose," her mother said vaguely as she dealt the cards. One child had always seemed enough to her mother.

Winter dusks. A triangle of figures playing cards, and then a pair. Or didn't they play after she went to college?

Oh, that endless first winter at college, when she used to trudge home from the library just as the chimes began to sing and Venus made a pinprick in the sky. Dusks when her face was slapped by the cold and the waterfalls over the gorges were frozen like people who die in the middle of a sentence, and she was lonelier than she had ever imagined she could be and all she had wanted was to sit within touching distance of a green velvet chair.

Mechanically she gathered her few belongings and put them into her suitcase. She stripped the bed and folded the sheets and blanket and piled them neatly at the end of the bed.

Why am I doing these things, she wondered, when I should be tearing my hair and sobbing? She wished they could have a funeral. But no — her mother's body was to be given to the hospital in which she had died. It was all in the will. No memorial service. Nothing.

"Funerals, cremations, services aren't for me," her mother had said after a close friend's funeral. The day stuck in her memory because it was one of the few times her mother had worn a hat.

She sighed. She would have to wait until she was in Paolo's arms. Paolo would help her. But who would help her father?

Quickly she walked back to the living room.

"I'm in here," he called from across the hall.

He was making their bed. She stood in the doorway, watching him pull the sheets tight as if it were a normal, rumpled double bed, as if one side had not lain unused for months.

"You're very efficient."

"You forget I was in the army a hundred years ago."

"No, I don't. But, Daddy" — she touched his arm — "are you sure you can manage? Oh, I don't mean beds and dishes and that." She looked around the room. "I . . ."

"I managed all the time your mother was in the hospital," he said brusquely.

"I know, but now I think you ought to come home with me, at least for a little while."

"No. I'm fine."

It was hard not to believe him. Then she remembered Paolo's voice on the telephone: "Bring him back with you. He can't be alone. Not now."

How she wished her mother had left some instructions — a letter or a conversation she could recall. But even if her mother had been conscious at the end, she hadn't been that sort of wife.

"What should you do with your father?" she could hear her mother saying in the tone used for stupid questions.

"Just a clue — where do you think he should be now?"

"Where he wants to be," her mother would have answered.

Now he was on the telephone in the living room. She lingered in their bedroom. Though her mother had not been here for months, the room had the faint, pleasing scent of the perfume she used to wear. It was an old-fashioned, very good perfume, new in the twenties, and her mother had never been tempted to change.

"It reminds me of my flapper days," she used to say as she sat before the antique mirror and her child watched her, wondering why the image wasn't as pretty as her mother's face and arms.

Suddenly she was filled with a childish desire to spill the perfume over her neck and arms. Her mother wouldn't mind, she was sure, but her father might. Besides, what was the point?

"I made a reservation at Antonio's. I think we'd better go," he said when she went back to the living room. She nodded, biting her lip, wishing she could say what she wanted to: that he shouldn't have made a reservation at such a small place where they were always warmly welcomed, that it would be a ghastly meal, that the waiters and owners (who all seemed to belong to one enormous family) would never understand why they were eating out when they should be grief-stricken at home. She knew she was right but somehow she couldn't speak. She felt as if he had taken her hand and they were running with her big bird kite, both of their hands on the reel. He was such a marvelous kite flier; they always got theirs up and it soared way above the others.

"It's the running," he used to say, so pleased as they watched it. "You have to watch the wind and decide which way to go and then run like hell."

They walked leisurely along Madison Avenue, a tall, graying man and a young woman — obviously his daughter, she thought as she caught their reflection in the window of a chic dress shop that had replaced one of her mother's favorite flower markets.

"That's nice." She pointed to a purple and white print.

"Paolo would like it," he said, which meant he didn't. He thought her clothes weren't feminine enough but he couldn't believe she had taste so different from her mother's, so he blamed her way of dressing on Paolo. She smiled and took his arm.

"Don't get fat," he said.

Their eyes almost met; she was an inch or so shorter. Now he looked happy. She felt herself loosen. This afternoon she had felt as if her muscles would be permanently taut. Yet here she was, only a few hours later, walking easily, though the soft asphalt sometimes caught her heel, though her mother was dead.

Near the restaurant he stopped and started to say something, then checked himself. He let go of her arm and walked in first. At any other time that might have seemed like rudeness; now she thought he was taking a moment to tell Antonio what had happened.

Once inside, she felt her ears pound: "She's the same," her father was saying to Antonio's anxious eyes.

"Ah, you are tired, my dear?" Antonio took her arm. He had known her since she was a child. He had watched her on countless Christmases and birthdays (her parents had no family in New York so they used to save Antonio's for special occasions) and now he was holding her arm on the evening of her mother's death and he didn't even know it. There was something cruel about it. Grief as well as happiness must be shared. That seemed one of the elementary rules of life. She felt like an accomplice to a crime. She wanted to grab her father's arm and get out of there; instead she let herself be seated.

"I didn't want to spoil our last night together," her father said when Antonio had left their table. "I'll come in tomorrow and tell them."

His concern for her was so genuine that she knew it would be pointless to argue that you didn't do this, that there was something immoral about it, that they should never have come here tonight — who was hungry anyway?

No, she couldn't say it, so she chose merely to play an old tune between them.

"Your generation hates unpleasantness more than it loves the truth," she said quietly.

Instead of answering, as he always did, "That's because we've known so much more unpleasantness than truth," he shrugged and grinned to make her laugh. She could feel the familiar melting sensation she remembered so well from childhood. So she smiled back, though she thought he was dead wrong.

But, she reminded herself, it worked the other way too. When she had told them she was going to marry Paolo, he had been disappointed. He had higher hopes for her than a poor college instructor with a foreign accent. He probably would have liked to dissuade her, to try to explain the pitfalls of such a marriage, but he didn't. He arranged a huge wedding as if she were marrying the son of one of his clients. And when Paolo's parents came from Italy for the wedding, he greeted them warmly and was very gracious to them. She remembered how happy Paolo had been. Yes, she could forgive her father.

As they talked he jotted down the names of things the children would like. "It's been so long since I've been able to think of them, it's a luxury," he said, putting the list into his billfold. "Now tell me about Paolo."

She told him of the summer grant, the paper on Ariosto, the book on Renaissance poetry Paolo was editing.

"It's a pity your mother never knew he got tenure."

She nodded. The letter had come a few days ago, but by then her mother had not known them. She closed her eyes, seeing her mother's wan skin, her mother's lips drawn across her teeth in a scar of pain. And never a complaint. But why so much pain, why that strange face surrounded by her mother's hair? Why? It whirled around in her head until she felt herself struggling to get up. Her father's hands were clamped on her wrists.

"Don't, little one." She stared at him. She hadn't heard that pet name for years. "Don't." His eyes were so weary that she sat back. He took her hands in his. "This little piggy went to market," he said and shook her thumb.

"It's not fair."

"Who are you to say what's fair?" He pretended to be intent on his little game with her hands.

"How can you be so passive?"

When he looked up she expected anger in his eyes. Instead there were tears.

"What can I do? What in hell can I do?"

She nodded dumbly as he excused himself and made his way to the men's room. In minutes he had aged. He held his head bent to one side and his walk had the peculiar flat-footedness of the old. He was so tired. She knew from the nurses how often he had slept in a chair in her mother's room, unable to leave her; how often he had fed her mother and changed her, almost as if he couldn't bear to have anyone else handle her. He was exhausted and she was abusing him. Her skin turned to gooseflesh in shame. She would insist on taking him home with her. In her head she saw him stretched on the hammock between the maples in the garden. He could get lots of sleep; she would make his favorite foods; somehow they would get through the next few weeks together.

When he returned to the table he was his erect, smiling self.

"Come home with me," she started to say. "It will be easier if you're there."

He shook his head. "You'll be fine and I have piles of work waiting for me at the office. I've been away a long time." It was true. And perhaps he would be more comfortable in his own home. Then she remembered the asters waiting for her mother and knew he shouldn't go back there alone.

"Paolo told me to bring you home."

"I'll be fine," he said calmly. "I might even become a good cook."

For the rest of the meal, which, to her surprise, she enjoyed (the stomach doesn't know of death or grief, she conceded), they talked about some of the details that needed doing.

"The man from the *Times* wanted a picture, so I gave him this." He handed it to her. It was a photograph Paolo had taken last winter of her mother watching the children's Christmas play. A happy smile played about her mother's lips, but her eyes were pensive — was she beginning to feel the pain?

"It captures her quite well," he said. She nodded.

"And she liked it." He put it away. He was so casual. What did it matter which photograph? People might read the obituary: the wife of a prominent lawyer, a well-known authority on American architecture who had given her time to the boards of a great museum and a great hospital . . .

What did they know? she thought bitterly. And he was pandering to them. She put her cup down so abruptly that the coffee spilled.

He smiled as she wiped her fingers. "Don't be so angry.

As long as there's going to be a photograph, it might as well be a decent one."

She shrugged, once more ashamed.

"Don't forget to call Harry and Sylvia tonight," she reminded him, "and the Rosses and the Hillworths and . . ." She ticked off a few more names, but she knew from the way he was nodding that he wouldn't call anyone. Her parents had never needed their friends as much as their friends had needed them. They had always seemed content to be alone — never ungracious to others, but never actively looking for company either. During the winter, particularly, they would wrap themselves in a cocoon of work and their child and each other.

Your friends will be hurt if you don't, she wanted to say. But she couldn't push him anymore. Besides, here was Antonio.

"Everything satisfactory?" he asked.

"Of course, Antonio." They got up from the table. "A lovely last meal. Alexandra goes back to her family tonight. As a matter of fact," her father checked his watch, "in about an hour."

The station, usually so quiet at this hour, was swarming with people. They had forgotten it was Labor Day weekend.

"You'll never sleep," he murmured as he lifted her suitcase onto the narrow Pullman bed.

"I'll be fine, but what about you?" Her eyes searched his.

"I'll be fine, too. Doc Forstman gave me some sleeping pills. That will be a new experience, won't it?" He grinned.

"Practically LSD for you." But he didn't smile.

"We'll call you Sunday morning." She tried to sound casual. Then they kissed and he squeezed her hand and left. She went to the window of the compartment so she could wave good-bye, when suddenly he was back, his face looking drawn, as it had for those few minutes in the restaurant.

"What is it?"

"Nothing." He clasped her upper arms. "I just wanted to make sure . . . You'll be all right, won't you?" He looked at her intently.

She nodded, waiting for him to explain. But he simply dropped his arms and left. When she next saw him he was waving good-bye and blowing a kiss — his usual station parody of Cary Grant — as the train pulled out.

Slowly she undressed. Like a scolded child she carefully folded each article of clothing and laid it at the foot of the bed. She felt like wood. She put on her nightgown and turned down the bed and got in without bothering to brush her teeth. All she wanted to do was to sleep and sleep and sleep.

When she turned on the light she saw she had slept only three hours. She stretched and tried lying on her side, but it was uncomfortable, so she lay again on her back. She was grateful for the limitation; her father wasn't so lucky in that wide double bed. Was he restless, or had the sleeping pills worked? She tried to imagine him sleeping, and then realized, startled, that she had never seen him sleep. How strange! She thought of Paolo curled up on the living room couch on winter afternoons, and how one of the girls usually covered him with the afghan, and how they all took it for granted. Yet she had never seen her father take a nap.

The machinery of the train made a steady chugging noise, just as the children's books said. Perfect lambs:

> *I never saw a moor,*
> *I never saw the sea;*
> *Yet know I how the heather looks,*
> *And what a wave must be.*

> *I never spoke with God,*
> *Nor visited in heaven;*
> *Yet certain am I of the spot*
> *As if the chart were given.*

The first poem she had memorized when she was about ten. How astonished she had been when she learned that Emily Dickinson had really never seen the sea. Now the poem went round and round, stuck in her head.

She thought of the children. Maybe now that she no longer had to stay home, waiting for a call, they all could go swimming or for a hike before school started. When she called them this morning her older girls had been terribly upset. Ma-Ma, as they had called her mother, was their favorite person.

As the children did she thought of the coming months by the holidays — Thanksgiving, Christmas, Easter. Her father would come up for them. At Christmas he would stay a week, till after New Year's. He would read by the big stone fireplace, marking with his red pencil, and the children would bring him hot cider, and he would smile and look like himself again. Time — that was all he needed.

She shook her head as she often did in these conversations with herself. No. The only way he could be happy was if her mother had lived. They had been so close, so dependent on each other. They had always reminded her of the identical twins she had studied in Psychology I, halves of one personality.

But there was his work. He was so able, so well known. Didn't that count for something? And what about her and Paolo and the children? And her parents' friends? Now, after so many months, he could enjoy them; he would have more invitations than he could handle. He will get used to it, he will make a new life, his intelligence will see him through. He's still young — only sixty-five . . .

Sixty-five, sixty-two, forty, thirty-five, nine, seven, two. She recited all their ages in time with the pull of the train. Added up, they had been two hundred and twenty. Now they were one fifty-eight. Sixty-five, forty, thirty-five, nine, seven, two. Two, seven, nine, thirty-five, forty, sixty-five. Over and over she counted until she dozed a little. She woke and then dozed again, and soon a watery dawn light came through the crack in the curtains.

She stepped off the train, looking toward the big trees near the station house. The children usually hid behind them and came out with great ceremony — sometimes Peter Rabbit and his sisters, sometimes Pooh and his crowd. This time Paolo was alone, running toward her, holding her tightly in his arms.

"Where are the kids?"

"The Rackmans called and asked if they could go swimming and picnic for breakfast. You don't mind, do you? He looked as if he suddenly realized he was depriving her of her children.

"Of course not." There was an awkward pause. He had stepped back to look at her. They walked slowly to the car and sat in the front seat, not yet ready to face the phone or their neighbors.

"It's good to be alone with you," she finally said.

"Was there much pain at the end?"

"Hard to know, with all the drugs. I don't think so."

He seemed comforted. Her mother in excruciating pain had bothered Paolo more than anyone else. It was almost too much for him to bear. She and her father had become more resigned. Death means pain, cancer means pain. It was the lack of recognition the last few days that had been so horrible. Someday she would tell Paolo, but for now it was something only she and her father shared.

How tired Paolo looked. There were new lines around his eyes, and though he was a little sunburned, he looked pale. She touched his cheek. He took her hand and kissed it.

"So, what about Fa?" he asked, using the children's pet name for her father.

"So, what about him?" she countered, afraid he was going to say she should have brought her father with her.

"What will he do?"

"He'll go on living — go to his law office, see his colleagues and friends, catch up on his concerts, theater, museums, galleries. Buy beautiful flowers, look dashing, come up here on holidays, get fat on my marvelous cooking and impress the law professors here with all his knowledge and . . ."

Suddenly she was sobbing in Paolo's arms, sobbing as she had wanted to since her mother's bony hand had fallen away from hers just a little more than a day ago. He let her cry and cry and cry. Oh, the relief of it! It was so much more sensible than all that pretending. Paolo held her for a long time, until finally her body stopped shaking.

"What will he do?" she asked.

"I don't know," Paolo said, "but I do know that he won't manage at all well, that it will be hard. I don't know how long he'll last or how he'll try to kill himself — maybe he will drink himself to death — but however it is, we will live through it."

Paolo could never lie to her. She should have known that. And because he was speaking the truth, he said it as matter-of-factly as if he were reciting the marketing list.

Then he shrugged and turned in the driver's seat and started the car. As he drove along the familiar flat road home he put his free hand on hers.

Chairs
for Angels to Sit In

The House of Her Childhood

The house of her childhood is still standing. People named Wechsler live in it now.

"Do you want to see it?" her mother asked when she came home for a visit.

"Okay," she said. But the house they showed her wasn't her house. The rooms were not the same shapes, the walls were painted garish colors, even the built-in cabinets in the breakfast room and den looked different.

"It's still a nice house," her mother said as they got into the car. She smiled. It was a nice house; the children and father of the family had always known that, and since her mother's memory had chosen now, finally, to forget the times when she had hated the house, when she had wanted something bigger, something on a better street, something with a more imposing entrance, and, once, a ridiculous house with fake Georgian pillars, she, the daughter, was not going to remind her.

It had been a lively house, a contented childhood. People didn't seem so angry then. Children stayed close to home until they were quite grown. The wrenching away, the truth-seeing had come later, after her marriage, after her parents had moved into an apartment where she always felt she was an impartial visitor.

Yet, for years after she left it, for years after they left it, the house of her childhood was a presence in her life. Now and then she dreamed she was living in it with her husband, but those were vague dreams, bare outlines. Later, after the children were born, the dreams were more detailed and frequent. When the children were sick she dreamed they were propped up against the curved maple headboards of the beds she and her sisters had slept in. She was taking their temperatures in the drafty white-tiled bathroom, running up and down the wine-carpeted stairs, making tea and honey in her mother's wood and yellow kitchen. When her husband was thirty-five she dreamed a party, but it was not in her ranch home. It was in the old gray-shingled Colonial with the wide front porch and the living room that was simply the large space that came after the front door. People were drinking and talking, not in the garden she had spent the last ten years planting, but in the narrow deep backyard whose flower beds were always wild and raggedy, whose patio had cracked green and blue slates, and whose main attraction was a huge wisteria with pendulous, almost sickenly fragrant purple blooms. In the winter the crying of her babies came slowly in her dreams, as they wound through the halls of the old house, so that when she woke it was with a strange disoriented start, then utter relief that she was in her cozy bedroom with the children around the corner and that she could run barefoot to them without half freezing to death.

"Why do I keep dreaming about us in that house?" she asked her husband. He didn't know either. After she had dreamed of undressing with her husband on a hot summer's night in her parents' huge bedroom, she became frightened. There must be some deeper meaning to these dreams; she would go to see a psychiatrist.

Of course she didn't. Someone got sick, or needed orthodontia, or the water heater broke. Besides, now that the children were getting older, the dreams came less often. They were also more manageable, her whole life was more manageable. While the children were in school she spent the mornings writing.

She bought the paper a ream at a time.

"What are you writing? A book?" the man in the stationery store asked.

"Not yet, just stories," she answered.

"Children's stories?"

"No, grown-up stories."

He shrugged. "So much paper for stories?"

One day she saw a painting hanging on the wall of a friend's apartment. Although it was actually a painting of the apartment in which it hung, it was the living room of the house of her childhood. The same blues and grays and wines, the same-shaped furniture, tables, lamps. The painting had a window that overlooked New York City, but the room was a living room on Long Island in the forties and fifties.

"I'm keeping it for the artist. She's a young friend of mine, in her twenties. She lives in Maine," her friend said.

"Is it for sale?" she asked.

"Yes, I think she wants six or seven hundred dollars."
How discouraging. She could never afford that.

Her friend said, "You can send her a little each month, I
know she has made that arrangement with other people."

"No, I can't afford it," she said.

Soon after that she dreamed that her father was dying —
in his bedroom in the old house — and that she and her
husband and children were crowded into the other three
bedrooms. Her mother wasn't there. The winter was bitter
cold, the house icy, the air gray. The children were sick a
lot, their misty vaporized rooms steamed all night. Her
father was hooked to a large machine. Even the old oak
tree that the town had cut down to widen the street in
1955 was there; it arched over the double window. In the
mornings when she went to open the curtains, her father
whispered hoarsely, "Sometimes I think I am staying alive
just to watch that oak."

Even her husband thought it was a crazy dream. And he
was not one to put much stock in dreams. Her father was
already in his office at 7:30 A.M. Her mother was opening
her eyes in her decorated bedroom. Her children and husband had slept peacefully in their snug, warm house. The
oak tree had been cut into lengths twenty years ago. As she
dressed that day she wondered, Am I losing my mind?

A few weeks later she saw the painting again. Her friend
told her, "The painter said if you're interested you can
have it for less. Four hundred dollars. And you can send it
to her when you have it." Immediately she felt better. She
took the painting home that day and hung it to the left of
the piano. In the morning the clean east light whitened it.
In late afternoon, when one or the other of her daughters

was practicing, either gentle dusk glowed upon it or, in the short dark days, lamplight flickered around it. The painter called the painting *Chairs for Angels to Sit In.*

Her mother said, "It looks like our living room in the old house." Her voice was full of surprise; she was really saying: Why do you want a painting of that old unfashionable furniture?

"Besides," she added "how could you buy a painting with a venetian blind in it when your father is in the curtain business?" The children rolled their eyes.

But they didn't like it either.

"It's not exciting enough," the eldest said.

"Why put a living room inside a living room?" the little girl asked.

"You can't see what's going on outside the window. What is going on out there?" the boy said.

Her husband smiled when he saw her looking at it. Which she did quite often. Her father didn't even notice it, then nodded after someone pointed it out to him.

A friend complained, "It isn't even signed. Why isn't it signed?"

None of that mattered. The dreams had practically stopped. She breathed easier. And on the first of the month she wrote a check for twenty-five dollars and sent it with a short note to the artist.

Finished. Done with. Or so she thought.

To her surprise the painter answered the notes. The young woman wanted to know more about the people who had bought her painting. She wrote back. She told a little about herself, her husband, her three children. But the artist wanted more. She wanted a correspondence, a *rela-*

tionship. At the beginning and end of her monthly and sometimes more than monthly letters, the artist wrote, "Why don't you talk to me?"

The nerve! She could feel herself getting angry. Why don't you talk to me? Indeed! She didn't have time to talk to people she has loved for years. How could she begin a correspondence with this artist? She wrote back trying to explain how busy she was, but the artist didn't want to hear. She was a persistent young woman. Why don't you talk to me? the artist kept writing.

So one morning she sat down at her typewriter and wrote:

SILENCES

I have two sisters, both of whom I love. One lives nearby, we see each other often. We talk, we laugh, we yell at each other sometimes. The other sister lives two hours away by car.

"Hello, love," she says when she calls on my birthday. "How are you? Phil? The kids?"

"Fine, and Larry and the boys?" I answer. Then we talk, but awkwardly. It is as if at the beginning of our lives we had so many words allotted for each other and now we have begun to run out. When I hang up I am defeated. Nothing that I feel has gotten through to her. And she will never know that my nightmares are often about something terrible happening to her.

My aunt died of a stroke at forty-nine. When I called my uncle whom I don't know anymore but whom I loved as a child I said, "How are you managing?" A long pause. "Are you there?" I asked.

"I'm here." He hesitated. "I'm trying to find the words to tell you how I am." They came out one at a time. "I feel lost. I go from room to room looking for her. I imagine I see her walking on the street and run to catch up with her. Some days I think I'm going crazy." He stopped. "I come home from work after half a day because I can't concentrate. This has never happened to me before. And the children are no help. They want people, lots of people."

I thought he was finished, then somehow I knew he had decided to tell me more than he had told anyone else. Neither of us knew why. Maybe because I believe so much in words he knew I would guard them, remember them. Anyway, he said, "She talks to me in my dreams. When I wake up and look in the mirror I can see that I have been crying."

For a special project in the seventh grade my older daughter wanted to visit the special education school at Grasslands. Some of the children are Mongoloid, some retarded, some have marked physical problems like epilepsy, others are disturbed.

"How much can you take?" the principal asked my daughter and her friend. They answered wisely: "Middle of the road."

"Smart girls," he said. He called in a teacher and the girls went on their tour.

Then he turned to me. "Would you like to see a class?" I

nodded and knew without asking that he was going to show me the most seriously damaged pupils. Only four kids were in the classroom. It was 11 A.M. and the teacher looked exhausted. Two children sat at a table playing with Fisher-Price toys, one was singing to himself. A few feet away a girl in a wheelchair whinnied occasional high sounds. But the one that attracted everyone's attention was a magnificent black child whose eyes pierced you when they looked at you. He sat at the end of the table apart from the others.

"He's the son of an eminent professor at Harvard," the principal said. "He has never spoken. Every test shows that he is capable of speech, but he is autistic. His parents are African. They are grateful we have gotten him to sit still for about two minutes at a time and look directly at another person. When he came to us he spent most of the day crawling up the walls like a monkey."

"But he's so beautiful," I whispered.

"Yes, he is." Now the principal's voice was not so matter-of-fact, his face sagged a little.

Later in the day I called an old friend. I could not get that child's face out of my head; even now, three years later, it often returns to block my vision.

"They're crazy," my friend said impatiently when I told her about the child. I listened because she knows a lot about special education. "Africans don't have autistic children," she said.

My son has lost his walkie-talkies. Gone. Disappeared. Nothing is ever stolen in our neighborhood, and I suspect they will turn up when we begin to rake leaves.

"I know it's my fault that they're gone." My son wets his lips as he always does when he is saying something he has rehearsed in his mind. "And I know I don't take such good care of my things, but I really would like to buy another set, with my own money" — he slips that in quickly — "because I miss hearing the policemen talk. I really do." I use my gesture for "we'll see" and suppress a smile. He thinks I am laughing at him and begins to cry.

"I really got used to hearing the policemen!" he flings over his shoulder as he goes down the hall to his room, "and I miss them!"

Voices of people I miss: old friends, teachers, couples who are divorced and never together anymore except in my head. A boyhood friend of my father's says, "So, where are your stories. I'm waiting."

"I have copies, I'll send them to you," I assure him. But he is dead.

A long time ago I loved a very angry man. Sometimes I think he is the angriest man in the world. Everyone was afraid of him. Except me. And when I learned I could make him smile and laugh and speak in a soft warm voice I was very happy. So was he. But he wanted more than I could give him and I wanted more than he could give me. So we parted. And have not spoken since. I often wonder what he does with all that anger.

When I was a senior in college there was a couple who were graduate students in the English department. They were both tall and wore long green army raincoats. She was thin and elegant, even in army surplus. In my dreams

I think I look like her. They used to stride along, their long legs synchronized as they crossed the quad. I can still see them frowning and, occasionally, smiling at each other. I can't ever recall hearing them speak. If I didn't know better I might have taken them for unfortunate mutes who had to depend on subtler forms of communication than ordinary speech. If I shut my eyes I can see them handing each other candy bars — mostly peanut chews — with a tenderness that made you want to turn your head away.

Years later someone told me they were divorced.

"He decided he couldn't live on peanut chews, now he's a health food freak," the reporting party said.

We once had a black and white springer spaniel named Lilly. My husband was crazy about her. Every weekend he took her for a long run to the nearest county park. She loved to race across open spaces, and when those weren't available the local streets would do. When I opened the door she would dart out and in frustration (for our town has a leash law) I would call, "Lilly! Lilly!" in vain after her beautiful side-to-side gait. In a few hours she would return, not in the least remorseful, and I was so glad that the police hadn't found her I would hug her and praise her when I should have been disciplining her with a newspaper.

What we didn't know was that she was eating out of every garbage can in the neighborhood.

One summer day she was terribly thirsty. It was hot, but she was thirstier than she should have been. About four in the afternoon I gave her still another bowl of water. She lapped it up and looked at me sorrowfully.

"Oh, Lilly, what's wrong!" I took her head in my hand. "Please, please, tell me what's wrong!" I shouted. Her eyes rolled back, she was dead.

A neighbor had heard me and came running. Together we moved her into the shade and covered her. Two hours later my husband fended off the flies that had begun to converge around her and wrapped her up to take her to the vet for an autopsy. She was only four years old. He carried her, all sixty pounds of her, as tenderly as he had carried our tiny dead baby four years before.

When the vet called he was furious. "I found pieces of Lego, aluminum foil, slivers of tin, scraps of wool — you name it — in that dog's stomach. She died from a piece of toxic meat."

I read in the *New York Times* not long ago about a couple whose twenty-one-year-old son was murdered. Stabbed. By the deranged former lover of his girlfriend. The parents want to have the word "murdered" engraved on the tombstone. The cemetery authorities would prefer not to have it there. But the parents feel the truth must be told. The news report also said that a rabbi is going to help them try to convince the cemetery people they are right.

Why don't you talk to me, my murdered son?

Some nights when my husband comes home I am so tired I have no words left. I am happy to see him, but nothing comes out of my throat, and he sees my tiredness and doesn't press me into conversation but allows the children to interrupt. Sounds whirl around us. Blessedly. After the children are in bed I sit in the living room like a bunch of dried sticks. Listlessly I think I would be better off in bed, but it's too early. I'm grown now. So I read and he puts on some records and reads, too. After a while he yawns and stretches and puts on his jacket. He has to put the car away. I begin to play the piano, something I like to do late at night when I am tired. As I play my left elbow is only a foot from the painting, your painting, my artist friend whom I have not yet met. When I stop to take a new piece of music the dog stirs restlessly. I play once more and as I play I feel as if I have walked into the painting, that I am sitting in one of those comfortable, old-fashioned chairs, and that outside the window, far beyond the city suggested there, tall evergreens are pushing silently upward into a dazzling moonlit night.